JESSICA BECK

THE DONUT MYSTERIES, BOOK 30
BAKED BOOKS

The First Time Ever Published!

The 30th Donut Mystery.

Jessica Beck is the *New York Times* Bestselling Author of the Donut Mysteries, the Classic Diner Mysteries, the Ghost Cat Cozy Mysteries, and the Cast Iron Cooking Mysteries.

For all of you, my dear and cherished readers, from A to Z,
Thanks from the bottom of my Donut
Heart for coming along for the ride!

There's a new bookstore opening up across the street from Suzanne's donut shop, and when a group of mystery writers descends on April Springs for a panel on murder and mayhem in the book world, is it any wonder that homicide is soon on the menu at Donut Hearts?

CHAPTER 1

THE DARKLY LIT SPACE IN the back of the town's brand-new bookstore, The Last Page, had recently been painted a soft shade of yellow, but the hastily made sign on the door proclaimed that it was, at least for the moment, the Green Room. That had more to do with the visiting authors who'd come to town for the grand opening than it did the actual color of the walls. Inside the cozy area were four rigid chairs, a small table, and a cart strewn with cookies, assorted pieces of fruit, two bottled waters, and a few remaining treats supplied by Donut Hearts, the town's favorite donut supplier.

There was one other thing in the room as well, though the way it lay crumpled on the floor in one corner made it hard to see at first in the dim light of the space.

Was it a pile of discarded tarps from the painter's recent visit, or perhaps even a prop for the mystery-writing panel given not so long ago?

No, on closer examination, this was clearly no prop.

It was a body, and judging by its deathly stillness, a real-life murder had occurred once more in the sleepy little town of April Springs, North Carolina.

"Suzanne, are the donuts for my grand opening celebration ready yet?" Paige Hill asked me the second she walked into Donut Hearts just before eleven a.m. Paige was a slight, wispy blonde, almost elfin in appearance; somewhere in her late twenties, she had a resting face that always seemed to look pensive, not that it mattered at the moment. The young woman was clearly stressed about her new business venture opening, and I was going to do my best not to add to her already high level of anxiety.

"Paige, I won't make them until later this afternoon so they'll be fresh for the party, but I've got the final sample we worked up in back," I said. "Give me one second and I'll go grab it." Since eleven was our normal closing time at the donut shop, I locked the front door before going in the back to retrieve the promised goody. My shop had undergone a major makeover fairly recently, and though the events that had happened during the remodel had been rather tragic, I loved the results. On my way back past her, I asked, "Would you like something to nibble on while you're waiting, or perhaps some coffee?"

"Thanks anyway, but I couldn't eat a bite, and I'm hopped up on caffeine as it is."

"Too much coffee will do that to you," I said agreeably.

"It's not that. I bought a gallon of Trish's sweet tea from the Boxcar Grill this morning, and I've been sipping from it all morning. I swear, I can almost feel my teeth rotting as we speak, and my nerves are jangling more than a high school janitor's key chain."

I grabbed a bottle of water for her from the fridge and handed it to her. "Take it. It's on the house. Maybe you should get off the hard stuff while you still can."

Paige took the offering gratefully, and after a large gulp of water, she smiled at me. "Everyone here is so nice. I'm so glad I decided to open my bookshop in April Springs."

"I'm sure your aunt would be happy that you did," I said. Paige's late aunt, Naomi Bussbottom, had been a fixture in town for years; some thought she'd found the fountain of youth the way she'd remained so sprightly well into her nineties. Forgoing the usual methods of demise of her compatriots, Naomi had perished in a small plane crash, which she'd happened to be piloting herself just after getting her flying license. Paige had shown up for the funeral as Naomi's last living relative, and she'd shocked us all by taking her inheritance and opening a bookstore in one of Momma's empty buildings on Springs Drive across the road from Donut Hearts.

"You know, I wanted to call it Bussbottom Books, but calmer heads prevailed in the end," she said with a grin. "Aunt Nam loved her last name. Did you know that all three of her husbands demanded that she take their last names, but she refused every last one of them? It always gave her such great pleasure to inform people of it upon first meeting them."

"Your aunt was something special, all right," I said, remembering my many encounters with her over the years that always managed to leave me smiling. "Now, let me grab that sample donut so I can get your final notes on it."

I slipped in back, where my lone employee—who also happened to be one of my very best friends, Emma Blake—was finishing up the last batch of dirty dishes. "Paige is here to see the final version of the donut," I said with a smile.

"Oh, goody. I've got to see her reaction for myself," Emma said with a grin as she threw the towel she'd been using down on the counter.

I grabbed the sample donut and plated it before taking it out to the bookstore owner.

"She's going to love it. Suzanne, you've outdone yourself this time," Emma said happily.

"I appreciate your willingness to come back into the shop in three hours to make a new batch of donuts with me for the grand opening celebration," I told her.

"I'm more than happy to do it. I don't have any classes today, and Barton is working on a new dish for the hospital menu. He gets absolutely obsessed when he's concocting something. If I didn't know any better, I'd think the two of you were related."

Young Barton Gleason was a culinary master who just happened to work at the local hospital cafeteria, amazing visitors and patients alike with his stunning skills. He'd been all set to move to Charlotte when Emma had caught his attention, and he'd suddenly decided to stay in April Springs at the last minute, much to all of our delight. Barton was one of the good ones, and I had high hopes that he and Emma would work out. "Because of his culinary genius or his sparkling personality and rapier-like wit?" I asked her.

"Sure, let's say all of that is true and leave it at that," Emma said with a laugh.

My assistant and I walked out front, and we presented Paige with the donut, making sure that the little candied dagger was plunged deeply enough into the raspberry-filled donut to produce a suitable amount of dark-red ooze on the top around the blade.

Paige's face lit up when she saw it. "It's perfect! Where on earth did you find that tiny little dagger, Suzanne?"

"It's amazing what kind of confections you can order online these days," I said. "Are you sure it's not just a little too..."

"Gruesome?" Emma supplied. "Ghastly? Murderous?"

"You haven't met many mystery writers, have you?" Paige asked us both with a grin. "The audience and the panel members will all love these treats, and I'm betting they will be the talk of the grand opening."

"How did you manage to get four well-known mystery writers to show up in April Springs for your opening, anyway?" Emma asked. "Brad Winslow has got a pretty big following, but the other three aren't exactly rookies."

Paige frowned for a moment before speaking. "What can I say? I got lucky. They had a break in their schedule on their publisher's book tour, and they graciously agreed to come here without much notice."

There was clearly more to the story than that, but Paige was just as obviously reluctant to share it, so I didn't press her. "Well, however you managed it, I'm certain that it will be amazing."

"I hope so. I'd hate to think that I'm wasting Auntie Nam's money on all of this."

"I'm curious. Why did you call her Nam?" I asked her.

"It's simple enough. I couldn't say Naomi when I was a child, and of course, my quirky aunt was delighted with the new moniker. She was my great-aunt, actually. I hope she'd be proud of what I've done with her money. I'd like it to serve as her legacy."

"I'm sure she'd be honored," I said. "Now, back to business. If you approve the donut in its final form, Emma and I will start our production run at two, so the treats will be ready by five at the latest. When should we bring them over to the bookstore?"

"Please, come over whenever they're finished. I can give you both the two-cent tour before we open to the general public."

"It all sounds wonderful," I said. "I can't believe we're finally getting our own bookstore in town. It's a pretty incredible thing you're doing."

"I'm just going to be selling books. You two are the ones doing incredible things," Paige said as she admired the donut we'd created just for her. The young woman had a way of making Emma and me both feel as though we were the most important part of her celebration. When she smiled, it had a way of lighting up the room, and I was glad she'd decided to become a member of our community.

After Paige was gone, I asked Emma, "What are your plans between now and when we meet back here later?"

"I'm going to head home, take a shower, and then grab a nap, though maybe not in that particular order." Emma laughed. She sniffed her hair, and then she grinned at me. "Do you ever get tired of smelling like donuts all of the time?"

"I used to, but Jake loves it, so who am I to disagree?"

"How's he enjoying Raleigh?" she asked me.

"He claims to be homesick, but I can hear some of the delight in his voice about feeling useful again, even though he tries hard to disguise it."

"How long is he going to be gone?"

I shrugged. "That remains to be seen." Terry Hanlan, an old colleague of his with the state police, had gotten himself into a sticky situation with his personal life, and he'd called on Jake for help. It was a favor we'd both been more than happy for him to grant, since Terry had once saved my husband's life while they'd both been on the job. I didn't get a straight answer on what the two of them were up to at the moment, only that Terry had taken two weeks' vacation time to resolve a personal crisis and that he'd needed Jake's help. I'd most likely get the whole story when my husband came back, but for now, I was living by myself again. At least Grace was in town. Jake had only been gone three days, but Grace and I had already gotten back into our old habits of palling around just as we had when we'd both been single. Her boyfriend, Police Chief Stephen Grant, was tied up with a case of his own, a mysterious hit and run on the edge of town, which left us both free to do pretty much whatever we pleased.

"I know that must be tough on you. So, what are you going to do with your free time?"

"Actually, I was thinking about catching up on our inventory here," I said as I looked around. "But your idea sounds a lot better than mine. I believe I'll go back to the cottage and take a nap, myself."

"And the shower," Emma added. "Don't forget the shower."

I laughed at her as we finished our closing ritual for the day. Ten minutes later, we were walking out of Donut Hearts together.

"I'll see you soon," I said.

"You bet," Emma replied.

I headed back to the cottage I'd once shared with my mother and now my current husband and decided that Emma had indeed conceived of a perfect plan.

If I could manage it, I was going to try to get both a shower and a nap before I had to go back to Donut Hearts and start the entire process of making new donuts all over again.

CHAPTER 2

"I CAN'T BELIEVE WE'RE FINALLY FINISHED," Emma said as she rinsed the last rack. Even she sounded a little weary from the double session, and she was a great deal younger than I was. "Is it just me, or was this like the longest day ever?"

"It's been rough," I said, "but at least the donuts turned out beautifully."

"Should we stab them now?" Emma asked me as she lofted a tiny confectioner's butcher knife no more than two inches long over one of the filled donuts.

"Let's wait so all of the raspberry filling doesn't ooze out before the celebration," I said. Without the daggers and the subsequent graphic gore, the donuts seemed a little plain, so I could understand Emma's desire to make them complete.

"Okay, but I want to stab a few of them myself when it's time," she said.

"Wow, I didn't realize you had such a wicked streak in you." I laughed. "What did a donut ever do to you?"

"You have to admit that it's got to be satisfying plunging the dagger in," Emma answered. "I think we should offer more oozing donuts at the shop than we do now."

"Even one would be more than we sell right now," I said with a laugh. "Are you talking about special treats for Halloween?"

"Sure, why not then, too?" she asked with an evil grin.

"Well, we can't very well make them for Valentine's Day," I reminded her.

"I don't know, we could always offer little powdered cherry donuts with cupid's arrows stuck into them. They could be really cute."

"How would we explain them to our customers? If we put them out without some kind of clarification, it would look as though a tiny archer had gotten loose in Donut Hearts and started shooting up our offerings, slaughtering donuts left and right."

After frowning for a moment, Emma said, "Maybe you're right. I still think we should at least make some for Halloween. After all, it was *your* idea."

I knew she was trying to influence me by crediting me with coming up with the original idea, but I wasn't that gullible. "Talk to me about it again in September and we'll see."

"Sure thing, boss," Emma said with a grin. After putting the last bowl away, she asked, "How are we getting these to the bookstore? We're not jamming them into the back of your Jeep, are we?"

"No, I don't think they'd make the trip, no matter how short it might be. I figured we'd just use the carts we have and roll them back and forth. After all, the bookstore is just across the street. It should only take us two trips if we pack them right."

"Sounds good to me," she said.

We were just wheeling the first load of donuts out the front door when we heard a commotion across the street directly in front of the bookstore. Two men were having an argument, and it was loud enough for us to hear every word of it. They were so caught up in their confrontation that they didn't even notice that Emma and I were standing there listening to every word they exchanged.

"What's going on, Suzanne?" Emma asked me softly. "Do you know either one of them?"

"No, they're both strangers to me."

One of the men was tall and stately, with flowing brown hair and piercing gray eyes. The other was at least twenty years older, and though his hair may have been dark earlier in his life, it was mostly gray now. He was quite portly, and his cheeks were red, though I doubted it was from the slight chill in the air.

"Brad, I'm telling you for the last time, stop trying to make the rest of us look bad on stage. We're not going to put up with it anymore."

"Simon, it's not my fault that the three of you combined haven't sold half as many books as I have all by myself."

"Are you sure about that? I hear Alexa's book is going to make the *New York Times* bestseller list! When was the last time you made it?" Did he take a certain amount of pleasure in tweaking the other man?

Brad ignored the jab. "You should all be eternally grateful that I'm even allowing you to accompany me on this book tour." It was clear that the younger man had an ego the size of Montana, and he wasn't afraid to throw his weight around, either.

"Don't kid yourself. You need us every bit as much as we need you," Simon replied.

"You're joking, right? Why on earth would I ever need a washed-up suspense writer, a dowdy grandmother selling recipe books disguised as mysteries, and a woman with exactly one novel to her name? I've done venues alone before, and I've proven many times over that *I'm* the draw, not the three of you."

"We humanize you," Simon said, clearly uncomfortable with confrontation. "If it weren't for us, your rampaging ego would drive away every reader who even bothered showing up."

That must have finally struck a chord with Brad. He loomed over Simon, and in a softer voice we could barely catch, he asked,

"Did the others put you up to confronting me, or did you come up with it all on your own?"

"Stop seeing conspiracies where there aren't any," Simon snapped. "That's your problem, you know. You've been writing about the seedier side of life in your thrillers for so long that you've started to believe your own books."

Brad's lips narrowed, and his nostrils flared. It appeared that Simon had scored yet another direct hit. "My books *are* real. It's you mundane folks who seem like paper cutouts to me."

"I'm getting tired of having this argument with you," Simon said with a heavy sigh.

"Don't worry, it's the last time you'll have to have it. After tonight, I'm pulling out of this farce of a tour. We'll see how well you three little pigs do without me."

Simon's face fell. "You can't do that. We've committed to five more venues."

"Watch me," Brad said icily.

"Our publisher won't allow it," Simon answered. "You may outsell the rest of us, but we all signed the same contracts when it came to public appearances, and he's the one who put this tour together. I might not be able to make you follow through on your promise, but he surely can."

Brad laughed, though there was no humor in it. "It's so cute that you actually believe that, Simon."

"I'm not bluffing. I'll call John Rumsfield himself," Simon threatened. "Let's see how you like dealing with the owner of Starboard House himself. He'll set you straight."

"As a matter of fact, there's no need to call John. He's already on his way. Besides, I've got a contingency clause that if I'm feeling under the weather, I can cancel my part of the tour with twenty-four hours notice." Brad glanced at his watch, and then he added, "I've got three hours to spare as it is, so after tonight, I'm through with you clowns and this joke of a sideshow." After feigning a cough, he added, "I do believe I'm coming down with something. Oh dear. I hope it's not catching."

"You can't do that to us," Simon protested. Brad must have really been the draw he claimed, because the older author was clearly panicked by the idea of his fellow panel member's potential absence. "We came to this little one-horse town because you insisted. You can't just turn your back on us after we leave."

"That's where you're wrong. I'm here to pay off one last debt. After I leave April Springs, I'm heading back to my place at the lake, and I'm going to write another bestseller. You know how that feels, don't you? Or is your memory not that good anymore, atrophied along with your dismal writing skills?"

With that, the tall man started to stalk away.

But evidently we hadn't been the only ones eavesdropping on the argument. Another man who'd been lurking near the bookstore stopped Brad before he could get very far. He was a slim gentleman in his late forties, his hair graying at the temples and a pair of glasses perched on his nose. His designer suit was out of place in my hometown, and I wondered who he was. "Brad. Where are you storming off to?"

"John. You're early," Brad said, clearly surprised by his publisher's sudden appearance.

"Your message sounded urgent," John said. "I flew down as soon as I could. Now, what's this all about?"

"I'm not ready to discuss it with you just yet."

The publisher began to frown. "I came all this way, and now you're getting shy all of a sudden? What's going on, Bradley?"

The man clearly didn't like the use of his formal name. Brad took a step closer to his publisher before he said, "There's something you should never forget, John." There was nothing warm about the way he said his publisher's name. The two men had very similar builds, but their likenesses ended there. Brad continued, "When I signed my last contract with you, you were just renting me; you weren't buying me outright."

"What is that supposed to mean?" the publisher asked his author as he poked him in the chest with his left index finger. There was anger in his voice now but also a touch of fear.

Brad wouldn't explain himself any more, and as he walked away, Simon approached the publisher. "John, I need to speak with you."

"Not now, Simon," the publisher said, clearly brushing him off as he started to follow his star author.

"This can't wait. It's important," the aging suspense writer said, clearly screwing up his courage to have his say. He put a hand on his publisher's shoulder, who glared at him until he removed it.

"You need to watch yourself, Simon," John said. "You're on thin ice as it is."

"Why would you say something like that? My books are still selling, aren't they?" the man whined. "And so are Bev's, for that matter."

"Yes, but the real question is, are they selling enough? We both know that I can't afford to have any dead weight on my list."

"We're not dead weight," Simon protested, but it was clear his publisher's words had cowed him.

John didn't answer. He merely stared at Simon for a single moment longer, and then he turned his back on him, dismissing him entirely. He hadn't even looked around to see who might have witnessed their conversation. For that matter, neither had Simon or Brad. The three men had been so self-absorbed that Emma and I had gone completely unnoticed not twenty feet away, leaving us to wonder what we'd just witnessed.

"Wow, who knew that writers and publishers could be so full of drama?" Emma asked me after they were all out of sight.

"Why would you expect anything less from any of them?" I asked with a grin as we pushed our carts across the street now that the show appeared to be over. "Writers sit around by themselves all day and make things up, albeit spectacular things, and I have no reason to believe that the people who hire them are any less odd. How could they *not* be dramatic in real life?"

I glanced over to see where we were heading. Paige had installed a large banner welcoming everyone to the grand opening across the front of the old brick building, and just below the flapping cloth, I saw the quaint little sign announcing her shop. *The Last Page* was written in florid script as though it were an illumination hand-lettered by a cloistered monk, or whoever had done that kind of work back then. I could always ask my stepfather if I really wanted to know. He was a history buff of all kinds, so he might know, but what he really specialized in were old and cold murders. It might have seemed like an odd hobby for a man in his retirement, but it seemed to suit him just fine, since he was a retired police chief.

"I don't know," Emma answered. "I suppose I always pictured authors sitting around fireplaces in easy chairs lost in deep thoughts all of the time."

"That's a little romantic, isn't it?"

"I suppose. How do you picture them?" she asked me as we started pushing our donut carts around to the back of the bookstore as we'd been instructed to earlier.

"Not that I've given it much thought, but I guess I just figured that they'd sit in empty rooms banging away on keyboards all hours of the day and night. I'm sure that it's just a job, not that much different than what the rest of us do with our days."

Emma shook her head. "I refuse to believe that."

"Hang around for the panel tonight and ask them yourself, if you get a chance," I said.

"Are you going to the talk?"

"I hadn't really given it much thought, I've been so focused on making these donuts. I probably will, since Jake is out of town. It could be fun, especially if they all dislike each other as much as it just appeared."

"That's the spirit," Emma said as I knocked on the back door of the bookstore.

Paige looked frazzled as she answered our summons.

"You still want your donuts now, don't you?" I asked her.

The new bookstore owner seemed more than a little distracted by my question. "What? Yes. Of course. Bring them in." Doing her best to summon a smile, she added, "They look marvelous," as she looked over our offerings. "What about the daggers?"

"We'll bring them with the last load of donuts," I explained. "We wouldn't want your donuts to ooze out too quickly, would we?"

"No, of course not," she said absently. "They're going to be perfect."

"We're glad you like them," I said as we wheeled the first batch inside. She was really rattled. "Paige, are you all right?"

"Yes. Things are just a little chaotic at the moment, that's all."

"I'll bet they are," Emma said with a grin. "We just saw two of your writers and their publisher nearly getting into a brawl in front of the donut shop not ten minutes ago." She peered around to see if she could spot them up front. "Are the others already here?"

"No, I've asked all of them not to come to the bookshop until five minutes before the panel is set to begin. Who was fighting, do you know? I was told that the group's publisher might be here, but I didn't think that would be possible, since the man runs a pretty large publishing company. How he can just leave New York on the spur of the moment and come to April Springs is beyond me. John Rumsfield not only runs Starboard House, which is a pretty big deal in mystery circles since it's one of the last few large independent publishers, I've heard it said that he owns it outright, making him the last of a dying breed." Paige bit her lower lip, and after a moment's hesitation, she asked us, "Was Brad Winslow one of the writers, by any chance?"

"That's what the other fellow kept calling him. He was a tall, handsome man, and he seemed to have a bit of a mean streak in him. Does that sound about right?"

"That's him to a T. Who was he arguing with?"

"An older, portly gentleman named Simon," I said.

"That would be Simon Gant. Did you say the publisher was there, too?"

"He was. How well do you know them?" Emma asked her.

"I don't know Simon or John at all," Paige said with a frown, "except by reputation, of course."

"Does that mean that you know Brad, then?" Emma asked. "He's kind of handsome, isn't he?"

"I suppose some women might think so," Paige said, and then she bit her lower lip.

It sounded to me as though their acquaintance wasn't exactly a happy one, so I decided to leave it alone.

Not Emma, though. "So then, you do know him," she said.

I was about to warn my assistant to back off, but to my surprise, Paige nodded. "Unfortunately, I do."

"Are you two dating, by any chance?"

I wanted to scold Emma for being so presumptuous with our client, but Paige answered before I could say anything. "Not for a very long time. How did you know?"

"Honestly, I just took a stab in the dark," Emma said. She must have finally noticed the hint of sadness on Paige's face. "I'm sorry to be so nosy. I didn't mean to bring up a sore point for you."

"Don't worry about it," she said brusquely. "Brad and I are finished."

"Doesn't that make it awkward having him here, Paige?" I asked her.

"What could I do? It's something I had to risk, whether it was difficult for me personally or not. After all, he's here at my request. They all are, but Brad is the one who arranged it at the last minute."

"I don't get it," Emma said. "If you two are estranged, then why would you invite him to your grand opening in the first place?"

"Under ordinary circumstances, I wouldn't have dreamed of asking him to come, but starting up a bookstore from scratch is a great deal more expensive than I realized it would be. I need a smash grand opening, or I might not be able to keep my doors open for very long."

"I'm sure you'll be a hit," I said, doing my best to comfort her and, in the process, try to end this discussion of her love life and change the subject to a happier topic. "Now, where should we put these donuts?"

"How about if you just stick them over here in the corner for now," Paige said, pointing to one of the few unclaimed spaces in the back. "Before you go get the next batch of donuts, let's take that tour I promised you earlier, shall we?"

I wanted to see the bookstore, especially as a sneak peek before the rest of April Springs got a chance, but I could see that Paige was clearly being stretched to the limits without indulging us. "I'm sure you have more urgent matters to attend to than showing us around the place," I said, trying to give her an easy out.

"Nonsense," Paige said. "Honestly, I could use a break."

"Yeah, Suzanne. In a way, we're helping her by distracting her," Emma answered with a grin. "Lead on, Paige."

As we walked into the main part of the shop, I was amazed by the sight of so many filled lovely wooden shelves dominating the space. "Are these made of walnut?" I asked as I trailed a finger across a shelf.

"Yes. They're beautiful, aren't they? I don't even want to think about how much they cost me."

I didn't doubt it. I wasn't sure how much she'd sunk into her shop, but if those shelves were any indication, Paige needed to be a roaring success to even begin to recoup her investment. She certainly had enough inventory on hand to do it. The shelves were loaded with books, both hardcovers and paperbacks, and whoever had created the sign out front had used their lettering skills to pen individual genre sections as well. *Romance* was written in flowery script, while the overwhelming *Mystery* section was lettered in a gothic font just dripping with ominous portent. There was even a section of autographed books up front, and I was amazed by the array of signatures collected there. "How did you get so many signed books so quickly?" I asked her as I noted some very well-known names represented there.

"I lucked out there. A collector who haunted conventions recently passed away, and I bought the entire estate's book collection. It cost me a pretty penny, but I think it was worth it."

I picked up an autographed volume by a prolific mystery novelist and saw that the book was very reasonably priced. "Are you sure you're charging enough for this?" I asked her.

Paige laughed. "Are you kidding? From what I hear, the only valuable books he's written are the unsigned ones. He must have terminal writer's cramp from signing his name so much." She reached for another book as she said, "Here's a real beauty. I was tempted to keep this one for my own collection." She then showed us a hardcover by a long-dead author, and when I saw the price tag, I knew that Paige hadn't been shy about pricing things on the expensive side.

"Wow, that's a lot to pay for one book," Emma said, noticing it as well.

"You'd be surprised. I could get that, and a little more,

tomorrow if I were to sell it online, but that's so impersonal, don't you think?"

"If you say so," Emma said as she wandered off to the science fiction section, lettered in a rather futuristic print.

"Maybe this was all one big mistake," Paige said softly as she looked around the shop.

I patted her shoulder gently. "It's completely understandable. You've just got opening-night jitters. It's going to be fine," I said, hoping that I was right.

"Did you get nervous when you first opened Donut Hearts?" she asked me.

"You bet I did! I must have eaten three dozen donuts myself that day," I answered with a grin. "Just remember, every store that has ever opened has had an opening day. You'll manage just fine."

"Thanks," Paige said. "You'll be here tonight, won't you? I could really use a friendly face."

"Of course I will," I said, making my mind up on the spot to be sure to attend. "Don't worry. It will work out fine."

"I hope you're right," she said.

"I'm so sorry to interrupt, but I have a question, Paige. How are you, Suzanne?" the older woman with striking long gray hair asked me with a smile.

"I'm fine, Millie. How do you like working at the bookstore?"

"So far it's been great, and I just know that I'm going to love it. There's just one problem so far, though."

Paige frowned. "What's that?"

"I'm worried that my entire salary is going to be eaten up by my book budget," she said happily. "At least I have my pension to live on." Millie had recently retired as the high school librarian, and it had been a perfect fit for her coming to work for Paige.

"I'm sure we can work something out," Paige said with a smile. "What is it you wanted to see me about?"

"We're running out of room in our designated mystery section. May I cannibalize some of the space from the literary area?"

"That will be fine for now. I'm sure we'll be fine-tuning things here for quite some time, so no worries about tonight, okay?"

Evidently some of my advice had boosted her confidence. Either that, or she was pretending to be calm for her lone employee's sake.

"Yes, ma'am," Millie said with a smile as she quickly disappeared back into the shelves.

After Emma and I finished our grand tour, we retrieved the last batch of donuts as well as the candy daggers and delivered them safely to the bookstore.

"That's that, then," Emma told me. "I'm taking off now, if it's okay with you. The dishes are finished, and I'm ready for tomorrow."

"I'll see you at the grand opening, then," I told her.

"You know it. I wouldn't miss it for the world," she said.

After Emma was gone, I decided to slip away myself. I had time to grab another nap, and I had every intention of taking advantage of it. Doubling my duties for the day had worn me out, and if I had any hope of staying awake for the night's festivities, I needed some sleep.

On the way home, I took a chance and gave Grace a call. "Busy tonight?" I asked her.

"I was going to do some paperwork, so literally any distraction you can offer me will work," she said with a laugh.

"The bookstore grand opening is tonight, and I made some of the refreshments. Want to go?"

"Sold," she said. "I'll see you later. I've got to go."

"See you," I said, feeling better that I wouldn't be going to the celebration alone.

It was going to be fun hanging out with Grace.

I only hoped that Jake was doing okay.

I tried calling him, but it went straight to voicemail. I didn't feel like leaving a message. Maybe if I tried later I would, but for now, I didn't want him to know that I was concerned enough to call. I couldn't let myself get caught up in worrying about him. He was a grown man used to dealing with dangerous situations, and I had to trust that he could handle anything that came his way.

At least that's what I tried telling myself as I grabbed a light blanket and spread out on the couch.

Before I knew it, I was fast asleep, despite the thoughts flying through my head.

Evidently I had been even more worn out than I'd realized.

CHAPTER 3

"I S IT THAT TIME ALREADY?" I asked as I opened the door of the cottage, rubbing one eye and trying to stretch at the same time.

Grace was standing there smiling. "Sorry, did I wake you?" It was clear by her grin that she didn't seem sorry at all.

"No, I was already up," I said as I moved aside to let her in. Trim and as lovely as ever, Grace had been my best friend for as long as I could remember.

"Liar," she said happily, and then she stuck her tongue out at me.

"What are you so cheerful about?" I asked as I went into the kitchen to make a fresh pot of coffee. Only a strong caffeine injection would get me going after two naps in one day.

"We're finally getting a bookstore of our very own!" she said excitedly. "I don't know who said it, but there's a quote that says something like a town isn't really a town unless it's got its own bookstore."

"That's Neil Gaiman," I said.

"Wow, I'm impressed. A literate donut maker. Who knew?"

"I happen to love his writing," I admitted.

"How did you stumble across him?" Grace asked me.

"Someone left a copy of *The Graveyard Book* at the donut shop last year, and I fell in love with it," I admitted.

"Color me impressed," Grace said, and then she studied my attire. "You're not wearing that, are you?"

I'd changed into sweats and an old sweater of Jake's after my shower. "Why, don't I look stylish enough for you?"

"You look lovely," she lied again.

"Let me get a little coffee in me, and then I'll be ready to get dressed and go."

"You'd better hurry," she said. "I drove in past the bookstore, and there's already a line forming out front."

"That's good news for Paige," I said. "I just hope we made enough donuts."

Grace laughed. "It's not *all* about business, Suzanne. For once, forget about being a donut maker and let's just try to have some fun."

"I'll do my best, but I'm not making any promises," I said as I poured two cups of coffee and reluctantly decided to give one to Grace.

"That's the problem with you small business owners. You can never leave the office behind."

"You never have that dilemma, do you?" Grace worked for a large cosmetics company, and I doubted that she'd ever worked forty hours in a week in her life, let alone the sixty I used to put in on a regular basis before Jake came into my life and I'd scaled back my work schedule.

"No, ma'am. Once I'm clocked out, I don't give it another thought. Would you like some help picking out something to wear?"

I looked at her outfit, a stylish red dress cut above the knee and tight around the waist. She looked as though she'd just stepped out of a catalogue. "Thanks, but there's no way that I can ever compete with you."

"Suzanne, I only wish that I had your curves."

"You're welcome to them," I said with a smile. I was constantly a little rounder than I would have liked, but my figure seemed to please my husband just fine, so I'd stopped being so critical about it. Well, I was working on it, anyway, but old habits died hard.

I thought about picking out a dress myself, but honestly, I was more comfortable in jeans, and besides, no one would be able to recognize me, it would be such a rare occurrence. I compromised and picked out my nicest jeans and a top that Grace had gotten me for Christmas the year before.

"That looks wonderful," she said as I modeled the outfit for her. "That top in particular is smashing. I approve."

"Could it be because you bought it for me?" I asked her with a laugh.

"Hey, what can I say? I have good taste. Just look at my best friend. Now come on. Let's go."

I glanced back at the kitchen. "Should we get a snack before we go?" It had been a while since I'd last eaten, and I didn't think it would be fair to snatch one of my own donuts at the grand opening.

"Tell you what. Let's go to the Boxcar Grill after the talk. My treat."

"Sold," I said. "Are you driving, or am I?"

"It's a lovely evening. Why don't we just walk through the park? Besides, it might be tough finding a place to park if we drive."

"I'm game if you are," I said.

As we left the cottage and headed through the park, I could see immediately that Grace had been right. It appeared that Paige had drawn a big crowd for her grand opening.

I just hoped that it all went off without a hitch.

"Man, it's really packed in here, isn't it?" I asked Grace as we found a spot in back away from the temporary stage that had been set up in front.

"It's pretty crowded. I can't believe the fire marshal isn't shutting us down."

"No way that's going to happen. He's up front with his wife. If he was crazy enough to try to stop the talk, he'd be sleeping on the couch for the next ten years."

The man's wife was clutching a book fervently to her chest, and I could see that it was Brad Winslow's latest novel. There were quite a few of them in the crowd as well, but there were even more of Alexa Masters's only book. I had a hunch that if Brad saw that from the stage, he was going to have a meltdown. Even Simon Gant and Bev Worthington were represented in the crowd, but in far fewer numbers. I saw at least two dozen folks that I recognized and quite a few more that I didn't.

One of the ones I knew approached me, a cardboard box clutched to his chest as though it contained ingots of gold. "Isn't this exciting?"

"Abner, I'm surprised to see you here," I said. Abner Mason was a quirky fellow, and that was being kind. He was known for constantly jotting things down on napkins, old receipts, any scrap of paper he could find, and no one really knew why. Abner was a big man, a brute with heavy hands that were rough and calloused from his work on car engines.

"I wouldn't have missed this for the world. Tonight is the night that changes my life forever!"

"How so?" The man was as animated as I'd ever seen him in my life.

"I'm getting one of these writers to endorse my book," he said, stroking the box as though it were actually alive.

"I didn't know you wrote a book, Abner," I said, surprised yet again by one of my fellow townsfolk. It just proved yet again that there was more to most people than anyone ever realized.

"I know people around April Springs think I'm crazy with

my constant note-taking, but I've been writing it all down for years to use in my book, and it's finally finished."

"Is it a book of sayings or something?" I asked.

"No. It's a murder mystery," he said. "One day I'm going to be more famous than everyone here tonight. Just you wait and see."

"Well, good luck with that," I said, trying to figure out some way to disengage from the man.

He did it for me though, turning and leaving me without another word.

Grace tapped me on the shoulder as I saw Abner worming his way toward the front. "What was that all about?"

"Evidently Abner wrote a book, and he's going to try to get one of the writers here tonight to read it and endorse it," I told her, shaking my head slightly.

"That's not how that works," Grace said.

"I know that, and you know it, too, but do *you* want to be the one who crushes his dreams?"

"No thanks; not me," Grace said.

I continued to look around, and then I saw all three members of my book club sitting in the front row. I was happy to see that they'd all made it. I caught Jennifer's attention, and she nudged Hazel and Elizabeth, who all waved at me happily the moment they realized I had arrived. I'd told them about the bookstore opening during our last meeting the month before, and they were each as good as their word, coming out in force to support Paige, and to meet the authors, as well, I was sure. There was no doubt in my mind that Elizabeth would try to get each email address for her massive correspondence list, since she liked to collect writers like some folks accumulated coins or stamps.

As I continued to scan the crowd, I felt a tap on my shoulder. I turned to see Paige standing there with one of the men Emma and I had seen outside arguing earlier.

"Suzanne, this is John Rumsfield. He runs Starboard House Publishing."

"Actually, I own it."

"Nice to meet you," I said, offering my hand to him, which he reluctantly accepted, however briefly. It appeared that shaking hands wasn't all that common a practice for him. I'd seen him out in front of the bookstore earlier in the day, but I wasn't about to mention it, since he clearly hadn't even noticed my presence.

"Have you ever thought about writing a book?" he asked me pointedly.

"Excuse me?"

"I showed him your donuts," Paige explained. "He thought they were delightful."

"Love the dagger, love the blood," he said. "It would look great in print."

"It would have to be the world's shortest book though, wouldn't it?" I asked him, doing my best not to smile. "I wouldn't know where to begin writing a cookbook," I admitted.

Grace piped in. "I think it's a wonderful idea."

John glanced at her, and then he looked back at me. "I'm not talking about doing a cookbook. I'm looking to replace one of my culinary cozy mystery series."

I couldn't contain my laughter at that. "Thanks for the offer, but I honestly wouldn't know where to begin."

"I can find someone to guide you. It's not as hard as you might think," he said, glancing at the empty stage.

"I find that hard to believe."

"Mysteries with recipes are hot right now," he said. "No worries. Like I said, we'll get someone to babysit you."

The idea was insane by any reasonable definition of the word. I'd read more than my share of mysteries over the years, but I didn't have a clue how one might go about actually writing one, and it was sheer hubris for anyone to suggest that I could.

Was that what writers were to this man, interchangeable cogs in his publishing machine? "Thanks again, but I don't think so."

"Fine. Whatever. It was just a thought." Once I dismissed the idea, he appeared to forget that I was even there. "When does this thing start?"

"Right now," Paige said after taking a big gulp of air.

"Good luck," I told her as I patted her shoulder.

"Thanks."

Paige made her way to the front, and then she rapped a book on the table to get everyone's attention.

"Thank you all for coming tonight to the grand opening of The Last Page."

There was a smattering of applause, and after it started to die down, she continued. "Our goal is not only to bring you the books you want to read but to provide, on occasion, the opportunity to meet the men and women who write them. Without further ado, I'd like to introduce tonight's very special guests." She nodded to Millie Winesap, who was standing by the back room that was serving as a green room for tonight's special event.

"First, we have Simon Grant, author of *Midnight Mayhem* and many others. Simon has been published for over twenty years and has produced a string of fine novels we all know and love." The older man we'd seen fighting earlier came out from the back of the store and waved to the polite smattering of applause from the crowd. He frowned for a moment as he glanced around, and I had to wonder if he'd been expecting a bit more of a fuss or perhaps a longer introduction. I'd been to a few events in the past where the person introducing the speaker went on longer than the keynote address lasted, but clearly Paige wasn't of that ilk.

After Simon took his seat, Paige said, "Next, it is my distinct honor to introduce Bev Worthington, author of the *Cooking By*

Moonlight cozy mystery series featuring amateur sleuth Fanny May June. The series now stands at twenty-nine books, with number thirty coming soon." The applause was a little more enthusiastic this time. When she emerged from the back, Bev looked like everyone's ideal grandmother, with a ready smile and a lap big enough for three small grandkids at the same time. She took her place at the table with a soft smile for Simon, and a few words were shared between them that I was too far away from the stage to catch.

"Next, we have Alexa Masters, author of *The Last Death*, which was just today named a *New York Times* and a *USA Today* national bestseller!" The applause this time was thunderous, and I glanced over to see a svelte and rather attractive woman in her early thirties make her way through the crowd. Her long dark hair shone as though there was a spotlight on her, and she seemed a little overwhelmed by the attention as she made her way to the stage. I'd been expecting a little resentment from the other authors already seated, but they both smiled at her warmly as she joined them.

"And finally, last but not least, *New York Times* bestselling author Brad Winslow, author of *A Deadly Kiss*, *A Deadly Touch*, and *A Deadly Embrace*, to name but a few."

The applause this time, though robust, didn't match the greeting Alexa had just received, and that fact wasn't lost on Brad Winslow. His smile was rather terse as he made his way to the front, and I noticed that each of the other authors had strained expressions on their faces as he joined them, even Alexa.

Paige took her seat in the middle of the table, and the panel began.

There were fireworks from the very first question, and at one point, I thought two of the panelists might come to blows when Brad suggested that Bev wrote cookbooks that had a little mystery in them instead of the other way around. Alexa had to put a hand on Bev's shoulder to keep her from launching herself at the man, but Brad merely smiled at the older woman's reaction. I noticed that Simon got a few shots in at Brad in Bev's defense, and they finally shared a smile that made me wonder if the two older authors had gotten rather chummy on their tour.

The panel seemed to go downhill from there, and it was clear that soon enough, Paige had completely lost control of the event. Instead of stepping in to squash the authors when they started sniping at each other, she sat back and helplessly watched them increase their attacks until it seemed that they'd all lost sight of the crowd and why they were gathered there. Finally, the publisher, John Rumsfield, evidently had enough. Making his way to the front, it was obvious that he was going to shut the entire event down when Brad Winslow stood and did it for him.

"Ladies and gentlemen, I have some amazing news that I'll be sharing tomorrow at a press conference at Books of Wonder and Intrigue in Charlotte during a solo personal appearance that has just been scheduled. Trust me when I tell you that it will impact the future of my career, and I urge you all to attend."

With that, the author walked off the stage and out the front door without even a moment of hesitation. I'd glanced at John Rumsfield's face when Brad had made his announcement, and he'd gone pale upon hearing the news. He didn't go after his writer, though. Instead, he was frozen in his tracks by the announcement. Not so frozen was my new friend, the brand-new bookshop owner. I knew that Paige had scheduled a group signing after the panel, and she hurried after Brad Winslow, obviously trying to get him to come back in to sign books for his loyal fans.

We all watched out the window as he clearly refused her, and finally, she slapped his face over something he said to her! Brad shook his head, waved a hand in the air at her, and then he stormed off yet again. Paige looked embarrassed by the confrontation, but that was nothing to what she experienced when she realized that she'd had a rather large audience watch what had just happened. Doing her best to gather herself, Paige returned to the store, made her way to the dais, and then announced, "That ends our panel discussion. The authors will be available to sign their latest books, which we have on hand available for purchase. Don't forget, they'll sign two books you might already own for every new one you purchase here tonight. Thanks again for coming, and now let's give our writers the hand they deserve."

The applause was enthusiastic, and Paige nodded to Millie, who in turn signaled to a bevy of high schoolers carrying boxes of books by each author. She must have recruited some of her favorite students to help out tonight.

Grace pulled on my sleeve and asked with delight, "Can you believe that?"

"Which part, the feeding frenzy on stage or Paige's argument with Brad Winslow?"

"Take your pick," she said. Eyeing the line already forming up front, Grace asked me, "Are you buying a book?"

"I thought I would, but the lines are already getting kind of crazy. Even Simon has his own group of fans."

It was true, though the older man's line was quite a bit shorter than any of the others. Brad's absence was conspicuous, but most of them must have migrated to Alexa's queue, which was snaking through the store and out the back. Bev, whose line was quite a bit smaller than her younger counterpart, was making up for it by having long conversations with whoever happened to be standing in front of her. I noticed that the ladies from my book club had managed to grab spots near the front of Alexa's line, and Elizabeth was taking a selfie with her as we watched.

"Why don't we go get a bite to eat and come back when the lines have died down a little?" Grace suggested.

"That sounds like a plan to me," I replied. I found Paige at the register in front. "We'll be back in a bit. We're ducking out to get a quick bite. Can we get you anything from the Boxcar?"

"I couldn't eat anything if I had to," she said. "Did you see what happened outside with Brad? Of course you did. Everyone did! I'm so humiliated."

"Don't be," I replied. "After the performance Brad put on, nobody could blame you for what happened. I was surprised there wasn't cheering involved when you slapped him. What exactly did he say to you to elicit such a strong reaction?"

"I don't want to talk about it," Paige said, her face converting into a plastic smile as a customer approached.

"I get it. If you don't want anything from the Boxcar, at least have a donut," I said with a grin.

"If I get a chance," she said lamely, and then she turned to her customer.

Once we were outside, Grace asked me, "Is she all right?"

"Probably not, but give her a little time; she will be. I was a wreck when I opened Donut Hearts, and I didn't even have to deal with anyone else's ego but my own."

"You don't have to tell me. I was there, remember?" she asked with a smile.

"I do. Let's go eat before everyone else mobs the place."

"Sold," Grace said as we walked the three dozen feet to the Boxcar Grill.

CHAPTER 4

"**A**T LEAST THERE'S NOT A crowd here," Grace said as we walked into the diner to find it mostly empty.

"Not yet, anyway," I answered as Trish approached us, her ever-present ponytail bobbing as she walked.

"I'm surprised to see you both. I figured you two would still be at the bookstore," the diner's owner told us.

"We were there, and we're going back, but we wanted a bite to eat in between." I looked around the mostly empty dining room. "Wow, that grand opening really took a bite out of your customer base, didn't it?"

"Don't kid yourself. As soon as things wrap up over there, I'm going to be flooded with customers. I'm glad Paige decided to open her bookstore. That building has been empty for too long."

"Let's just hope she can stay in business," Grace said.

"Why would you say that? Did something happen I don't know about?" Trish wanted to know, eager for news, since she'd been at her diner during the festivities.

"Why don't you grab an extra sweet tea and join us?" I suggested. "We can bring you up to speed on what happened while we're waiting for our food."

"I don't mind if I do," she said. "What can I bring you two to eat?"

"I'll have a burger and some fries to go with my sweet tea," I said.

Grace grinned as she held up two fingers. "Make that two."

"How about three? Would you mind if I joined you? I haven't eaten yet myself, and I have a hunch if I don't do it now, I'll never get the chance," Trish said with a smile as she headed back to the kitchen to place our orders.

"We'd love to have you join us," I said, and Grace nodded in agreement.

Grace and I got settled in at a table near the front so Trish could watch the register, and five minutes later, the diner's owner came to our table bearing food and drink. "Here you go, hot off the grill," she said as she served us. "Now tell me what I've missed."

Once we finished bringing Trish up to speed on what had happened, she whistled softly. "Why is it that I always seem to miss out on the fun?"

"It's one of the perils of being married to your business," I said. "Don't you *ever* take any time off?"

"No, I'd miss it too much. I don't know how you manage leaving the donut shop in Emma's hands two days a week yourself."

"I don't know. Call me crazy, but I like spending time with my husband." Grace had finally found someone in the police chief and I had Jake, but Trish seemed to have the worst luck when it came to the men in her life.

"Where is your hubby, by the way?" Trish asked. "I haven't seen him around the past few days."

"He's in Raleigh helping out a friend," I said.

When Trish realized that I wasn't going to add anything more to the explanation, she asked, "I'm guessing he's not helping him move, is he?"

"I couldn't say," I replied.

"You can't, or you won't?" Trish pushed.

"If I knew, I might tell you, but Jake says it's all hush-hush, and I'm taking him at his word."

"Hey Trish, are these new placemats?" Grace asked, clearly trying to change the subject.

"The design is the same old one, but these particular mats have never been used before," she said, taking the hint. "They're nice, aren't they?"

It wasn't that I didn't want to talk about Jake. I just didn't know what was going on with him.

As the three of us ate, we explored a variety of other topics, laughing and teasing each other just as we had for years.

When it was time to pay the bill, Trish refused to provide one as she said, "This one is on me, ladies. I can't remember having so much fun."

"Then you really should get out more," I told her with a grin.

"Hey, I'm trying," she replied, and then she spotted Grace sneaking into her wallet. "No tips, either, young lady. Am I making myself clear?"

Grace looked a little embarrassed about getting caught. "Are you sure?"

"Positive," Trish said.

"Thanks, then."

As we left, Trish added, "There's just one more thing."

"What's that?"

"If something else happens over there tonight, come here and tell me about it immediately."

"It's a deal," I said, "but I have a feeling that the fireworks are all over."

Boy, did I ever turn out to be wrong.

The lines had indeed petered out to more manageable sizes by the time we walked back into The Last Page.

I looked around quickly and saw that there was still no sign of Brad Winslow, although the other three authors were doing their best to appease those who were still waiting for signatures.

I grabbed one of Simon's books, much to Grace's surprise. "Really? You're getting one of those?"

"I'm getting one of each of the three, but Simon doesn't have a line." Not only was it true, but the poor man kept glancing longingly at the women surrounding him. Alexa's queue was still rather long, and the poor women in Bev's line were being interrogated about what they loved best about her series before she'd sign a single book.

I slid the book in front of Simon, who looked a little surprised finding someone in front of him.

"I hope you enjoy this," he said as he signed his name in swooping great letters. "Shall I personalize it for you?"

"No thanks. Just a signature is fine," I said.

He pursed his lips for a moment before replying. "You're not one of those *collectors*, are you?"

"No, I just never cared for personalized books. Do you get a lot of them?"

"You'd be surprised," Simon said with obvious distaste. "They're vultures, you know."

I was surprised by the vitriol he showed toward someone who wanted to buy one of his books. "That's a little harsh, isn't it?"

"You might not be aware of it, but there is a faction of folks that loves to get signatures from older authors. They stockpile the books until that inevitable day when the writer passes away, and then they flood the market with autographed books, hoping to cash in on a moment of sentimentality. I chose my words carefully when I called them vultures."

"I didn't know that," I said as I took the book and headed back to get one of Alexa Masters's pile. "Thank you for signing."

"You're welcome," he said, trying to smile but having a difficult time doing it.

The poor man looked absolutely miserable, and what was worse, I couldn't think of a single thing to say to cheer him up.

There was one thing after all. "Have you tried the donuts yet?"

His face lit up for real for just a moment. "Paige is saving one for me. They look delightful. Are they as good as they look?"

"I sincerely hope so," I said, suddenly feeling more goodwill toward the man than I had a moment earlier.

I grabbed a new book and got in Alexa Masters's line. Despite being more popular, Alexa's queue was moving quite briskly.

Grace was just ahead of me. "What was that all about?" she asked softly.

"I'm not quite sure," I said.

"Writers," she said with a smile, as though it explained the man's odd behavior.

I decided to keep my comments to myself.

Grace got a quick signature from the rising star of literature, and then Alexa signed a copy for me as though she were on autopilot. The woman looked so disconnected from the event that I was worried about her. "Pardon me for asking, but are you okay?"

"What? I mean, pardon me?" She looked startled to get a personal question.

"I don't mean to be so blunt, but you look a little rattled," I said softly.

Alexa started to break down, just a little, before she reined it back in. "The truth of the matter is that it can all be a bit overwhelming. This time eighteen months ago, I submitted my manuscript to my publisher. Even in my wildest dreams, I wasn't expecting any of this."

"It must be like some kind of fantasy for you," I said.

"I suppose. I never wanted to be famous, you see," she explained. "I thought the book would come out, if I was lucky it might sell a few copies, and that would be that. I wasn't prepared for how the people around me would react to my success."

I actually felt bad for her. "Maybe it will get better."

"I know I shouldn't complain," Alexa said, putting on a brave face, "but all I really want to do is go home, forget about this side of the business, and try to write another book."

"It must be really difficult being so wildly popular," Bev said a little testily from her place beside Alexa. She'd clearly been listening in on our conversation.

Alexa must have realized the way she'd sounded, because the real woman I'd just seen vanished into the façade she'd been presenting to the world earlier. As Alexa slid the book across the table, she said, "I hope you enjoy it, and thanks for giving me a try."

I walked back to the stack of books and found Grace watching me. "How do you do it, Suzanne?"

"How do I do what?"

"While I was waiting in line, I saw five different people try to have a personal moment with her, and she brushed them all off. You say one word to her, and suddenly she's telling you her life story."

"I don't know. People seem to like talking to me."

"There's more to it than that, and you know it," Grace said.

"I care about their answers, I suppose. I actually listen to what they have to say," I said. I'd been asked that question before, and I never knew how to answer it. Maybe I just had one of those faces.

Bev's line was finally down to one, so Grace and I grabbed a book apiece and got in line. The older woman was just finishing up with the woman in front of her, and as she turned to leave, I could swear she looked relieved to get away.

Grace and I approached her together. Maybe it would shorten our time being held captive.

Bev Worthington looked delighted to see us, or so it seemed. "Ladies. There's no reason to crowd. One at a time, please!"

"We just couldn't decide who got to meet you first," Grace said, covering nicely.

I knew she was being sarcastic, but evidently it was completely lost on Bev. "How delightful. You remind me of Fanny and her best friend, Giselle."

"Who are they?" Grace asked without thinking.

Bev looked at her as though she'd just spouted high treason. "I take it you aren't a fan."

"No, but your books sound intriguing," Grace said, doing her best to look interested in the cover in her hands.

"They really are. I've read a few myself, and they are really delightful," I told Bev. It was true, to a certain extent, anyway. I'd read a pair of her books, and she told a good story, though I could see how some folks might think they were a little heavy on the recipes. Besides, the plots had been nearly identical. Offering recipes could be a trap. One of my favorite writers had loaded her first books with tons of recipes as well, but she'd decided to pare them down in later books, something I found much more pleasing to read. "I'm a fan of Fanny myself."

"How very nice of you to say so," she said with a smile, recovering her aplomb. "Let me tell you about their latest dilemma. Poor dear Fanny has really gotten herself into a fix this time. You see..."

Paige took that moment to interrupt, bless her soul, before we got the next book's outline, which I had a suspicion would be oddly familiar, if the other two books I'd read were any indication. "I hate to break in, but we'll be closing in five minutes, and we'd love it if you could all sign some stock for us."

"Certainly," Bev said. She gestured to the untouched stack of Brad Winslow books. "What are you going to do with those? It would serve him right if you sent them back."

"I'm hoping he'll come by and sign stock before he leaves town," Paige said.

"Good luck with that. The man is a beast, a true beast."

Instead of replying, Paige turned to us. "Ladies, thanks again for coming. Millie will be glad to ring you up."

"Of course," I said.

"Suzanne, do you have a second?" Paige asked me as Grace and I started for the cash register.

"Of course."

In a low voice, she said, "I just wanted to thank you for everything. Your donuts were delightful, and having you here eased my nerves more than I can say. I was pretty rattled earlier, and I don't know what I would have done without your support."

"I didn't do anything. Really," I said.

"You did more than you realize," Paige said.

"Then I'm glad that I could help."

Bev coughed loudly behind us. "About that stock," she said.

"Coming," Paige said, pasting on a brave face as she turned back to one of her attending authors.

Grace and I paid for our books and accepted the nifty little cloth bags that were being supplied free of charge announcing the store's presence in April Springs, and we made our way home. It was late spring, but the weather still wasn't sure how to react. It would be chilly one moment, and the next, it would feel as though summer was indeed just around the corner.

"That was fun," Grace said as we walked along Springs Drive toward our homes. This time we'd chosen to take the road, since it had grown dark while we'd been inside the bookstore.

"And entertaining as well. I'm sorry Jake and Stephen missed it."

"Me, too, but we both know that they would have been fidgeting before it even got started. Do you have any plans for tomorrow?"

"No, not other than making donuts. How about you?"

"I'm not planning on making donuts at all," she said with a smile.

"You're really funny, aren't you?" I asked sarcastically. "Are you working?"

"I've got a meeting in the morning, but I'm free after lunch. Why don't we do something crazy and fun?"

"Sounds good to me," I said. I missed Jake when he was gone, but it was a good time to catch up with Grace, and I aimed to take advantage of it.

After she went into her house, I walked the final steps to my cottage, marveling at how my life had changed over the years, coming full circle to living back in the home where I'd grown up. The cottage was a happy, safe place for me, and I was forever grateful to Momma for giving it to us. Having Jake there with me only served to make it better. Whenever I went to my happy place when things were going wrong, it was always to the cottage, with the image of a fire blazing away in the hearth, cookies baking in the kitchen, and the company of those I loved that renewed my spirit.

How fortunate I felt being able to live it every day.

CHAPTER 5

AFTER I GOT READY FOR bed, I decided to take a chance and try calling Jake again. He'd warned me that he most likely wouldn't be able to answer his cell phone, but I decided to try anyway. He didn't pick up again, but at least I got to hear his voice, inviting me to leave a message. This time I decided to say something instead of just hanging up.

"This is your wife. I hope you are safe and well. I miss you. Tonight at the bookstore was fun. You would have hated it. Give Terry my love. I'll talk to you later. Good night. I love you."

It wasn't as good as a direct communication would have been, but I still felt better letting him know how I felt.

I went to sleep feeling warm and safe, ready for what tomorrow might bring.

At least I thought so at the time.

It was chilly when I went out to start my Jeep the next morning. I probably should have just walked, but I liked the short drive to work, and besides, it was awfully dark out. A path through the park that seemed so open and pleasant in the light of day could be absolutely ominous in the middle of the night, which was when I always went to work.

I drove the short distance to the shop and started to park when I noticed something odd at the bookstore across the street.

The front door appeared to be open.

Had Paige forgotten to shut it, let alone lock up on her way out? I couldn't imagine anyone breaking in and trying to steal a book, not that at least some of them weren't quite valuable in their own right. How would a thief go about fencing one, I wondered? I parked the Jeep in my usual spot and grabbed the big flashlight I kept tucked under my seat. It not only served to illuminate everything around me when I needed it, but it was stout enough to use as a club, something I'd proved firsthand in the past.

"Hello? Is anyone there?" I asked as I got to the door, but not poking my head inside. I started to think that maybe I should call the police. I always hated it in mystery novels when the heroine took her life in her hands doing something foolish, and it would gall me to die that way in real life.

I was about to hit 911 to get someone else there when I could swear I heard the sound of someone in trouble coming from inside. Was I right, or had it just been my imagination? For all I knew, the sound could have even come from *outside* the building, but my nerves were jangling like power lines in a high wind, and I wasn't going to take the chance that I was needed and stand there doing nothing just because I was afraid.

I had to find out what was going on inside.

I rushed into the bookstore before I could chicken out, flipping on the lights and dialing 911 as I went.

"Could someone come out to The Last Page immediately? I was driving by and saw that the front door was standing wide open. When I moved forward, I could swear that I heard someone inside, though I could be wrong about that part."

Before I could explain any further, the police dispatcher asked, "Who is this?"

"It's Suzanne. Suzanne Hart," I said impatiently.

"Hey, Suzanne. It's Glenda James."

Glenda was an old friend of mine, but I hadn't heard that

she'd joined the force. "Glenda, I didn't know you were a cop. I'd love to talk about it later, but could you send somebody out here right now? I think someone might be in trouble." So far I hadn't seen anything amiss in the store. Had I actually heard something earlier, or had it just been my overactive imagination?

"I'm not a police officer; I'm just manning the phones while Henry is out on a call. They were short staffed, and I offered to pitch in. You said that you heard noises. Is someone in the bookstore?"

"I don't know. I'm checking it out right now," I said softly.

"Suzanne, I'm no cop, but I know enough to realize that you shouldn't be in there alone. Let me get you some help."

"I can't just stand around if someone's in trouble," I said. "I have to see if I can help."

"Just give me a second, okay? I'll see if I can get Henry on the radio."

And then my cell phone went dead. Evidently Glenda hadn't mastered the art of putting a call on hold quite yet.

I didn't have time for this foolishness. I started to put my phone away and check out the two main back rooms when, to my surprise, my phone rang.

After I answered it, Glenda said, "Sorry about that. My finger slipped. Let me try that again."

Once more I was cut off.

I was just glad this wasn't a real emergency.

When my phone rang yet again, I said, "Glenda, just let him know I'm here."

"Give me one more chance," she said, and then I finally made it to hold after all.

Four seconds later, she came back on the line. "Henry will be there in one minute. He said to hold tight. Would you like to chat while you're waiting?"

"No, thanks. I'm good."

"Okay then. Oops, I've got another call. Bye."

I put my phone away and said loudly, "Is anyone here? It's Suzanne Hart." Why hadn't I bothered identifying myself when I'd first walked in the front door? There were only two main spaces left besides the restrooms—the back storage room and the break room that had been temporarily converted into a green room for the authors. I checked the storage room first. It was full of boxes and supplies, and I doubted that there was any way someone could be there without me seeing them.

That left one last large space, and I felt a knot in the pit of my stomach as I opened the door and flipped on the light.

At least I tried to.

Either the light was burned out, or someone had disabled it.

I was glad I'd thought to bring my big flashlight with me. Flipping it on, I used its bright beam to try to light up the room well enough to see inside. Evidently, Paige's supply of books had been too large to be held in one spot alone, because some of them had drifted over to this space. Four rigid chairs and a small table took up some of the free space, and I saw a cart with leftover cookies, fruit, some bottled water, and a few of my dagger-donut treats.

I was about to give up when I noticed something in the corner near a pile of books stacked haphazardly near one wall. At first glance, it looked as though it might be a pile of discarded tarps from the painter, but as I got closer, I got a sinking feeling in the pit of my stomach.

My flashlight had no trouble lighting the scene.

It was a body, and what's more, as I knelt down to check for a pulse, I realized that whoever had died was now cold to the touch. How long had the body been lying there?

Studying the scene with the aid of my flashlight, I saw that someone had taken a geode bookend, its ragged edge of crystals jutting out like broken glass, and they'd smashed the publisher, John Rumsfield, in the head with it.

The man was beyond my help, and it was starting to look as though the noise I'd heard had all been in my head.

Unless I missed my guess, he'd been dead for some time.

CHAPTER 6

WHERE WAS HENRY? HE SHOULD have been at the bookstore by now, but I couldn't do anything but wait on him. I considered going back outside, but I just couldn't bring myself to do it. As I knelt there, I noticed that one book in particular was near Rumsfield's right hand. Evidently his index finger had been dipped in his own blood, and I felt a chill run through me. The title of the book was *Seven Deadly Mushrooms*. It was a field guide to poisonous fungi. Had the publisher been trying to stand after being struck by the deadly bookend, or was there more of a message there than that? Out of habit, I took a few photos of the man, the bloodied bookend, and the marked book, and I was just putting my phone away when I heard someone calling out from the front.

"Suzanne, where are you?"

It was Stephen Grant, my friend and the chief of police for April Springs.

"I'm back here," I called out. "Someone's been murdered."

I saw a bright flashlight beam light up the hallway, and when Stephen came to the break room, he asked, "Why is it still dark in here?"

"The light's not working," I said.

I was about to show him John Rumsfield when his flashlight beam caught the corpse. "What happened?" he asked as he knelt down to check for a pulse.

"If I had to guess, I'd say that someone hit the publisher with that geode bookend a few hours ago," I said.

"How do you know who he is, and what makes you think it didn't just happen?" Stephen asked as he knelt down beside me to check for a pulse himself.

"I met him earlier at the bookstore opening, and as for the second part of your question, he's been dead for some time, hasn't he?" I asked Stephen. "The body's quite cold. Am I right?"

"Yes, I'd say so," the chief said as he stood, lending a hand to me after he was upright again. I was about to protest that I didn't need any aid when I realized that my knees had suddenly gone weak.

"Are you okay?"

"No, but I will be. I really hate finding dead bodies," I said flatly.

"And yet you persist in doing it," Stephen said, not unkindly but not exactly compassionately, either.

"It's not my fault!" I snapped at him.

"Hey, I'm on your side, remember?" he asked calmly as he reached for his radio to report what I'd found.

"Sorry. I'm just a little jumpy."

"There's no need to apologize. Why shouldn't you be on edge? I'd be a little worried about you if you weren't, to be honest with you." He then spoke into his radio. "Glenda, I want everyone up and at the bookstore in ten minutes, or I'll know the reason why."

"You want me to wake everybody up?" She sounded incredulous at the very idea.

"That's exactly what I want, so make it happen."

He turned back to me after he was finished with his temporary dispatcher. "Before everyone else gets here, take a second and tell me what happened."

"It's simple enough," I said. "I was on my way to work this

morning when I noticed that the door to the bookstore was standing wide open."

"You should have called us and waited for someone to show up," he said, chiding me a little.

"I started to, but then I thought I heard someone inside that might need help, so I came straight in. The truth is, given the circumstances, I would have done the exact thing all over again, given the chance."

He nodded, conceding my point. "Were the lights on or off when you got here?"

"They were all off, but I turned them on as I came in, so that explains why they're all on now. I called 911 the second I started exploring, but Glenda had some phone problems, so I wasn't sure I was going to get any help. I couldn't just ignore someone in trouble, Stephen."

"I get it. Believe me," he said sympathetically. "What do you suppose made that sound? There's no way the victim made any noise, and I doubt the killer would hang around after the murder."

"I'm beginning to think that it was just my imagination," I said. "Anyway, I searched the bookstore, and I found him back here. It had to be a crime of passion, wouldn't you say?"

"I'm not ready to say anything quite yet," the chief said cautiously.

"Come on. You and I both know that it had to be spur of the moment. Why else use a bookend that was already here? If someone came to town planning to commit murder, they wouldn't wait to find a murder weapon until they got to the bookstore."

"Suzanne, I appreciate you calling this in, and I'm glad that you're okay, but I'm going to handle this myself, okay?"

"Is that a polite way of telling me to buzz off?" I asked him with a hint of a smile. It was all that I could muster at the moment.

"I suppose it is. I don't mean anything by it, but things are going to get crazy here pretty soon. Why don't you go over to the shop and start on your morning donut routine? It might help take your mind off of all of this. That is, if you're planning to open despite this. If you want to shut down for the day, I'm sure everyone will understand after what you found here."

"No, I need my work to keep me occupied. If I go home to the cottage, I'll be all by myself, and that is something I just can't handle right now."

"Where's Jake?" he asked me, sincerely curious.

"He's giving Terry Hanlan a hand in Raleigh," I explained.

"Got it. I'll come over to Donut Hearts when I get a chance."

"Thanks. I'd appreciate that." I looked down at the body one last time before I left. "You know, he wasn't particularly nice, but he didn't deserve that."

"Very few people do, and yet it happens all the time," the police chief said.

"Too much, if you ask me," I said.

"Agreed," Chief Grant said.

As I walked out of the bookstore, Henry finally showed up. "Where were you?" I asked him, maybe a little too tartly.

"There was a prowler at Mrs. Blakely's place, or so she claimed," he said. "It was her third false alarm in four weeks, but she wouldn't let me go. Sorry I didn't get here sooner."

He clearly felt bad about leaving me hanging in the wind. "It's okay. John Rumsfield was well beyond any of our help when I got here, so you wouldn't have been able to do anything for him, either."

"I'd better get inside," Henry said before pausing and looking at me. "Suzanne, you don't look so good. Are you going to be all right?"

"Once I get the cake donuts started, I'll be better," I said.

He looked at me oddly, but he didn't ask for an explanation. As Henry went inside to join his boss, I hurried across the street to start my day, albeit a little later than normal. After unlocking the door and stepping inside Donut Hearts, I carefully locked the door again behind me, took three steps, then returned and checked it one more time. I had every right to be paranoid, and I wasn't about to beat myself up about it. Had I heard anything inside the bookstore, or had my curiosity about what I might find behind the open door supplied a phantom sound that gave me a reason to investigate? I honestly couldn't say, but I wished that I hadn't heard it and that I'd been able to stay outside and wait for the police to show up. Maybe then I wouldn't have the image of the publisher's body just lying there on my mind now.

I *hated* stumbling across dead bodies, but it had happened entirely too frequently in my past for my tastes. Would I ever be able to free myself from murder, or was I forever tied to a string of dead bodies that would lead me one day to my own grave? They were dreary thoughts, but they matched my mood perfectly.

I had two choices. I could curl up in the corner in a ball and try to come to terms with what I'd just seen, or I could make my coffee and donuts and try to salvage some kind of normalcy in my day and try to put John Rumsfield out of my mind.

In the end, there was really only one choice when it came down to it.

It was time to make the donuts.

I did give myself one allowance. Instead of leaving the front dining area dark as I usually did, I flipped on all the lights before turning on the coffee pot and heading for the kitchen to flip on the fryer. I didn't care what my power bill was going to look like that month.

I needed light around me, and lots of it.

I was just adding the first of the cake donut batter to the fryer when Emma walked in. "What's going on over at the bookstore?" she asked me.

I didn't want to tell her, since her father ran the town's only newspaper. I wasn't sure Paige's bookstore could overcome the scandal of hosting a murder on its first day of business, and having Ray Blake broadcasting it wouldn't help matters. Then again, it would be public knowledge soon enough, and I doubted that anything Emma's father printed could hurt any more than the rumors that would soon be flying around town. "A man named John Rumsfield was murdered there last night."

"That's terrible," Emma said, stumbling back against the counter.

I nearly forgot to flip the donuts now bobbing in the hot oil. They required constant attention, and if I didn't watch them, they'd be burned on one side and raw on the other. I had three minutes before I dropped the next batch in and Emma had to retreat to the front, so I talked quickly. "He was the man who published all of the visiting authors last night. Apparently someone hit him in the head with a geode bookend."

"How do you know all of that?" Emma asked me in wonder.

"Lucky me. I'm the one who found the body," I admitted.

Emma walked straight to me and hugged me, an awkward move since I was still holding the batter dropper in one hand. "Suzanne, are you okay?"

"I will be. Thanks for asking. You want to call your father, don't you?" I asked her.

"I won't do it if you don't want me to," she said.

"No, go on. He has a right to know. I've got to pull these donuts out of the oil and drop in another batch, anyway. Just make sure he pays you a finder's fee for the story."

"Oh, Mom will see to that," Emma said. "Thanks."

"It's fine. Now scoot. I have to get back to work."

"I started to say that I can't believe you're making donuts after what just happened, but I realized how foolish it would sound. They take your mind off what you saw, don't they?"

Emma knew me better than most folks did. I nodded, and she offered me one last look of sympathy before scooting out of the way. I'd let the dropper slip only once since I'd owned the donut shop, but I'd left the indentation in the drywall to remind me of how deadly the tool could be. The raised donuts were cut with aluminum wheel cutters that weighed just a few pounds each, but the dropper could do some serious damage if it hit someone.

After the cake donuts were finished, I called out to Emma, who must have been standing by the kitchen door waiting for my signal. "All clear. Did you call your dad?"

"He should already be over there," my assistant said with a nod. "Let me get started on those dishes." As Emma rounded up the things I'd already used, she said, "We don't have to take our break outside this time if it's going to bring up bad thoughts for you. I can't imagine the police leaving the scene any time soon."

"Thanks for offering, but if it's all the same to you, I'd like as much of our routine to survive as possible." It was a poor choice of words, saying *survive*, but I couldn't take it back. Soon the dough for the yeast donuts was resting, and most of the first round of dishes had been done. I set the timer telling me when it was time to come back to start on the dough again, and Emma and I headed outside after grabbing our coats and a pair of mugs full of hot coffee.

Hopefully, things wouldn't get any worse than they already were.

But only time would tell.

CHAPTER 7

RAY BLAKE WAS WAITING ON us the moment we walked outside.

Emma said, "Dad, what are you doing here? I thought you'd be at the bookstore by now."

"I couldn't get anything good out of those guys, so I thought I'd join the two of you. Suzanne, I'd love to hear your firsthand experience about finding the body, but first, is there any chance I might get a cup of that coffee you two are drinking? It's kind of brisk out this morning."

I wasn't in the mood to speak with the newspaperman about what I'd seen, but I couldn't be blatantly rude to him, especially in front of his daughter.

It turned out that I didn't have to.

Emma put her cup down on the table and walked toward him. "You need to go."

Ray looked surprised by his only child's reaction. "Come on, Emma. Don't be that way. I'm not hurting anyone here."

"I called you so I could give you a tip about the murder, not to have you come over here and harass my boss. I meant what I said. Look at my face. Is there any doubt in your mind that I'm serious?"

"It's okay, Emma," I said. "You don't have to protect me." I didn't want to cause any trouble between the father and daughter, so if it came right down to it, I'd rather answer Ray's questions, though it did make me feel good seeing Emma standing up for me. I knew it wasn't easy for her, and I was proud of her for doing it.

"I know that, but this is out of line, even for him," she snapped before turning back to her dad. "I mean it. Go."

"Fine," Ray said, holding his hands up in the air in his own defense. "I'm just trying to get a story. That's all. It's nothing personal."

"That's where you're wrong. It's all personal," Emma said.

"You don't have to tell your mother about this, do you?" Ray asked.

"I'm not sure what I'm going to do right now," she replied.

Ray shrugged, shot me a hapless smile, and then went on his way.

"You didn't have to do that on my account," I said. "I can handle your father."

"I understand that, but you shouldn't have to handle him at all. He has no right taking advantage of the fact that I'm his child."

"Are you two okay?" I asked her. I'd never seen her take such a strong tone with her father.

"I'm fine," she said. "Dad should know better, and Mom told me that if he ever got out of line again, it was okay for me to spank him."

"If you ever decide to do that, I don't want to be around to see it," I said with a smile, trying to diffuse the tension.

"I meant it figuratively, not literally," Emma answered, grinning in return as well. "I don't care what he does after Donut Hearts is closed for the day, but I won't have him accosting you during our break." She took a deep breath, and then she added, "Let's just forget he even came by, okay? You know what? I love the way the air smells this time of year."

"I'm a fan myself. I wonder if it's going to rain."

Emma took another whiff. "It wouldn't surprise me in the least. Suzanne, are you okay?"

"I'm fine," I said automatically, taking another sip of coffee.

"This is Emma asking, not Ray's daughter," she pushed a little harder. "You can talk to me."

"I'm so used to denying that I'm having a hard time with something that it's become a habit for me. Honestly, I'm still a bit shaky," I admitted. "It's an awful thing finding a body like that, and I hope it never happens again."

"You've had more than your fair share of it over the past few years, haven't you?"

I nodded. "It's kind of crazy, isn't it? Let's talk about something more pleasant, shall we?" I asked her.

"That sounds great to me."

"I've been thinking that it might be time for us to do another promotion at the shop. Things are starting to slow down a little as the weather gets nicer, so we should do something to give our sales a little boost. Do you have any ideas?"

"Boy oh boy, do I ever. Did you know that one of the big donut chains is doing a Pirate Day celebration every year?"

"I read about it online. We can't copy it, though. It will make us look as though we're trying too hard."

"I wasn't thinking that we should duplicate it, but how about having Halloween in May? Folks who come in dressed up can get a free donut, and we can have a contest for the best costume where the winner gets a dozen donuts on the house."

"Emma, we don't even do that much in October when it's really Halloween," I reminded her.

"That's what would make it even quirkier. Okay, if you don't like that, how about having a contest where our customers come up with their own donut ideas, and we make the winner?"

"That depends. Who gets to pick the winner?"

"We could do a poll at the shop. Something like 'buy a donut, get a vote.' It could generate some foot traffic and revenue and give us some fun too, coming up with a way to make the winning treat."

"I like that a lot," I said, "and I think the costume party idea in May has potential, too. You're getting pretty savvy, young lady."

"I can't help myself. It's all of these business classes I'm taking," she admitted. "Every time I read a case study about something someone has done out in the real world, my thoughts go immediately to how we could apply it to Donut Hearts."

"I have a feeling I should be contributing to your tuition, since I'm getting such good ideas because of it," I told her.

"No, ma'am. However, if you feel like bumping my wages a bit, I wouldn't say no."

I smiled when I saw her grin after she said it. "Let's see how your two new promotions go first."

"It's a deal," she said. "I've got files and files of ideas, and not just for the donut shop."

"What else do you have in mind?" I asked her.

"Barton keeps talking about opening a little café someday, and if he decides to ever pull the trigger, I want to be ready to help him make it a success."

"You two are really getting along quite well, aren't you?" I asked just as the timer went off.

Emma grinned. "I don't have to answer that, since I was just saved by the bell."

"Or the beep," I replied.

"Whatever," she answered happily.

She didn't have to answer; I could see it in her smile.

We walked back into the shop, and after I handed Emma my nearly empty mug to wash, I started in on the next phase of making the yeast donuts. It was a longer process, and once upon a time I'd considered doing the cake and yeast donuts at the same time, but the truth was I wasn't that big a fan of multitasking, and besides, I only had so many pots and pans. Doing it the way I was doing it now meant that I lost an hour's sleep every night, but the system was working, so ultimately I'd decided not to change it.

There was a knock on the front door a few hours later, and I wondered who was so eager to speak with me, since we weren't set to open for a while yet. When I quickly glanced out the front door, I saw the police chief standing there, a grim look on his face if ever there was one.

I opened the door to let him in. "Hey, Chief. You look as though you could use a cup of coffee."

"I wouldn't turn one down," he said with a sigh.

"Have a seat. I'll go grab you one."

I poured him a cup and snagged a sour cream donut for him as well. It was his new favorite donut, and it delighted me to find another fan of them. For the hundredth time I thought about changing their name to something more alluring, since sour cream and donuts don't really seem to go together naturally. The donuts were absolutely delightful.

"On the house," I said as I slid the coffee and donut in front of him.

"You know me better than that," he said as he pulled out his wallet and put three ones on the table in front of him. "Keep the change."

"One of these days I'll get you to accept something on the house," I said, ignoring his money.

"Maybe, but that day isn't today. Thanks for calling the office when you got to the bookstore this morning. I'm just sorry Henry didn't get there sooner. We've already had a chat, so I can promise you that the next time, his response will be quicker than it was this morning, or I'll know the reason why."

"It's okay," I said, feeling bad for being the reason for Henry's admonishment.

"No, it's not," Chief Grant said, and then he took a long sip of coffee. "That's exactly what the doctor ordered."

"I kind of doubt that, but it does hit the spot, doesn't it?" I glanced over at the bookstore and saw that there were still a few official vehicles parked over there. "Is John's body still there?" I asked him softly, having a hard time imagining the bookstore without a murder victim in it.

"No, the coroner came by, made a ruling, and the EMTs took him away." He took a bite of donut and then another sip of coffee before he spoke again. "Evidently it was exactly as it appeared to be. Someone took advantage of that bookend and hit him in the head with it."

"Did he die instantly?" I asked.

"Why do you want to know that?"

"Don't play games, Chief, it's too late, or too early, however you want to look at it. I saw that bloody fingerprint on the book near his right hand, so I know you spotted it, too."

Chief Grant shrugged. "Sometimes I forget that you've got more talents than just making terrific donuts. The current theory is that he wasn't killed instantly. He most likely only had a few seconds of consciousness before he died. Oh, and about the light. Someone must have flipped the breaker. Either that, or the wiring is bad there, but that seems like a bit much to swallow. Whoever did it didn't want a casual observer finding the body right away."

"And yet they left the front door wide open," I said.

"Maybe they heard a noise, or something else spooked them. Who knows?"

"Do you think there's any significance to the book the publisher chose?"

"On mushrooms? I highly doubt it. It was more likely that he just grabbed whatever was in reach."

"Maybe," I said.

"You have a different theory?"

"I don't have *any* ideas yet," I said.

The chief pushed the plated partial donut away and looked at me wearily. "Suzanne, are you digging into this mess?"

"How can I not, Chief? I found his body. That makes it personal."

"I get that," he said. "To be honest with you, it might not be a bad thing if you snooped around a little, as long as you're circumspect about it."

"You know me, I'm always discreet," I said with a grin.

He laughed, but there was a hollow ring to it. "Yeah, right."

"Is there anything else you can tell me that might help?" I asked.

"Why not? The door lock was intact, so it wasn't a break-in. I had a man speak with Paige Hill, and she swore the place was locked up when she left, but I'm not so sure, unless someone was hiding in the bathroom waiting for her to leave."

"That's possible, you know," I said.

"I was just kidding," the chief said.

"What else could it be, though? It's pretty obvious that John Rumsfield knew his killer, isn't it? We also know that whoever did it was probably right-handed."

"What makes you say that?" he asked me, clearly curious about my question and, more importantly, my deduction.

"It would just make sense, wouldn't it? I saw the angle of impact, it was tough to miss, and it would be difficult to say the least hitting him like that from behind. The publisher must not have been expecting it, since it was a direct hit."

"And why would the killer be right-handed? Because Rumsfield was hit on the left side of the head. Very good. Yes, we managed to piece that one together ourselves."

"There's no shortage of suspects either, is there?" I asked. "It's a complicated case."

"We're putting together a preliminary list, but this is all brand-new to me," the chief said. "You and Grace were at the panel; none of my people were there. What are your thoughts?"

"Well, from what I've read, don't *many* writers dislike their publishers?"

"That's a little nebulous, isn't it?" the chief asked. "I'm sure that just as many *adore* their bosses."

"Maybe in general, but yesterday afternoon, Emma and I heard John Rumsfield arguing with Brad Winslow *and* Simon Gant. Not only that, but Rumsfield implied that Bev Worthington might have a reason to want him dead as well."

"Why is that?" the chief asked me, clearly surprised that I had so much to contribute.

"Brad was threatening him about something, and Rumsfield told Simon flatly that he and Bev were on their way out. Not only that, but the publisher approached me about writing a culinary mystery series at the talk. He said he was going to have a hole in his schedule, so I have a feeling that Bev knew her time was limited as well."

"The way you tell it, that just leaves Alexa Masters in the clear," the chief said.

"I wouldn't go that far," I countered. "I just don't know anything about her yet."

"Is that it? Paige didn't have any reason to kill him, did she?"

"Why would you ask me that?"

"Well, to start with, it happened in her bookstore," he said.

"What would her motive have been?" I didn't want to tell him about Paige's former affair with Brad Winslow, but I really didn't have any choice. "She used to date Brad, by the way."

"Really? I didn't know that." He sounded way too interested in the new information. "Could she have killed the man to protect him?"

"You didn't see her slap him like we did. I doubt they're still carrying on, but you never know though, do you?"

"We'll look into it," the chief said. "Is that all?"

"Yes. No," I added quickly, suddenly remembering another encounter I'd had the evening before.

"Well, make up your mind. Which is it, yes or no?"

"Could I go with a maybe instead? Abner Mason was at the signing," I told him.

"So? I know the man's a little odd, but that doesn't make him a killer."

"No, but he had a manuscript on him that he was going to show the writers on the panel. What if he found out that the publisher himself was there last night? If they had a fight, Abner might have taken the rejection personally. You should have seen him talking about his book. He was almost irrational when he told me about it. You might want to talk to him, just in case."

"My, you've been busy, haven't you? I can see that you have your teeth into this. Are you going to drag Grace into your investigation as well?"

I laughed at the question. "Have you ever known Grace to do *anything* against her will?"

"No, not for as long as I've known her."

"I can say the same thing, and I've been around her a lot longer than you have."

"Just try not to muck things up for me, okay? It would be embarrassing to have to arrest my girlfriend and my favorite donut maker for interfering with an official police investigation."

"We'll do our best," I said.

"Not to do anything questionable, or not to get caught?" he asked me before quickly adding, "Forget I just asked you that. I don't want to know. One more thing before I go. I'm not going to be able to keep the suspects here indefinitely. I figure I've got three days before they start leaving town, and there's not much I can do about keeping them here without any firm evidence."

"Is that why you're willing to take our help?" I asked him.

"Hey, I'm not proud. If Jake were in town, I'd ask him for help, too. As things stand, I'm thinking about bringing in the mayor, but I'm not sure I want to go there just yet."

"Why, don't you think George would do a good job? He was a great cop in his day, or so I've heard."

"That's not the problem. I'm just afraid that if I give him a crack to slip into, he'll be running my investigation and leaving me on the sidelines before I know what happened. Like I said, I'm not that desperate just yet."

The chief stood, and I saw that the job was aging him beyond his years. It was clear that he loved being in charge, but it was just as obvious that it was taking a toll on him. I wanted to say something to him about taking things a little slower, but I knew it would be pointless, so I decided not to. Instead, I offered, "I know you won't accept anything on the house, but I could fill an urn with coffee and bring some donuts over to your crew. Would you be okay with that?"

"I'm not sure," he said, though it was clear he was tempted.

"Come on. Let me at least do this."

"Fine," he said, finally giving in. "I'm sure they'll all appreciate it. I know I do."

"I'm happy to be of some service," I said.

After Chief Grant was gone, Emma came out of the kitchen. "Has he left yet?"

"You weren't eavesdropping, were you?" I asked her with a smile.

"I tried to, but this door is just too thick. Have you thought about replacing it with something that transmits sound better?"

We both laughed. "I just volunteered to take a dozen donuts and a pot of coffee across the street to the cops who are there working."

"That's a great idea. I know you're busy, so I'll be glad to do it."

"Thanks. I appreciate that," I said.

"Any word on what happened?" she asked softly.

"Not really," I said. "Nothing has changed. The publisher was murdered in the back room of the bookstore, and so far, there aren't any specific suspects."

"That sounds like a quote my father might get from a police spokesman," she said.

"Then by all means, be sure to share it with him," I replied with a smile as I started filling a large thermos. "Why don't you box a dozen assorted cake donuts and run everything over while I finish rolling out the yeast donuts?"

"Can do," she said.

After Emma was gone on her errand, I went back to my donuts, and as I worked, I couldn't help wondering who had killed the book publisher. One thing was certain; it appeared to have been a spontaneous act. Or was it? We'd discussed writers and their patterns quite a bit in my book club, and one of the recurring themes was how clever they were at planning murders. Had someone grabbed that bookend on purpose, counting on finding something in the bookstore to make the act look rash? I looked around my own shop and realized that the rolling pin in my hand would make a fine murder weapon, as one of its predecessors had indeed been used for in the past. There were also knives aplenty and other things that could be equally deadly. I tried to think of what I'd seen in the bookstore that might have been used as well, and I came up with half a dozen objects just off the top of my head. I wasn't sure what that said about me, and I wasn't completely positive I wanted to find out. Needless to say, if someone had come to the bookstore intent on murder already, a creative mind would be able to find something to use to commit the act, and if *anything* was true, it was that there was a good chance we were dealing with a creative mind.

Now it was just a matter of figuring out which one had used their wits to end the life of their deceased publisher.

It wasn't going to be easy, but I believed with all of my heart that Grace and I were up to the challenge if she agreed to join me in my investigation.

I couldn't imagine her saying no, but if she did, I had other folks in town I could call on, though it was too bad that Jake was away on business of his own.

Either way, I wasn't about to go it alone.

CHAPTER 8

W E SEEMED TO BE GETTING pretty popular even before we were open for business. At least that's how it felt when someone started knocking on the door twenty minutes after the police chief left. Had he forgotten something, or was he simply returning the thermos of coffee?

It turned out to be neither.

I walked out front and was surprised to find Paige Hill standing there alone in the darkness. She looked as though she'd been crying, but who could really blame her? Her dream of opening her own bookstore was quickly becoming a nightmare.

I opened the door and let her in. "Come in, let me get you a cup of coffee and something to eat."

"I'll take the coffee, but I couldn't eat a bite," she said. "Isn't it just awful?"

"It's pretty bad," I said, locking the door behind her. I grabbed her a cup, filled it with fresh coffee, and then threw in a donut to boot despite her protest. "Here you go."

She took them absently, and after taking a sip of coffee, Paige said, "I can't believe you were the one who found John. By all rights, that should have been me. They said there was no sign of a break-in, but I *know* I locked that door when I left. I just know it!"

"Could it have been Millie?" I asked her, wondering if her assistant might have come back for something later.

"No, right now I only have one key. The other is in my safety deposit box. I had the locks changed the second I bought the building, so I know there are no floaters out there."

"Maybe you missed someone when you locked up." It was time to check Chief Grant's theory that he'd supplied earlier. "Did you look in both restrooms?"

Paige clouded up for a moment. "You know what? I'm an idiot. I didn't check the men's room. That's a mistake I won't make again. What I can't figure out is why John was there in the first place after hours."

"Perhaps he was meeting someone," I said.

"And he chose to trespass at The Last Page? It doesn't make sense."

"It might have been the only place he didn't think they'd be interrupted. I don't know, it's a possibility," I said.

"Suzanne, you're going to look into this, aren't you? Promise me that you won't ignore this murder."

"I'm not quite sure what you're talking about," I said as evasively as I could manage. Paige hadn't been a part of our community for all that long. How had she already heard about my exploits as an amateur sleuth?

"Don't bother being coy. Nan used to revel in telling me all about you and your crack team of April Springs Irregulars. That's what she called your cohorts, you know."

"It's nothing as interesting as all that," I protested. "I *have* been dragged into murder investigations from time to time in the past, but not usually by my own curiosity."

"This is certainly not frivolous for you, is it?" she asked. "After all, you found the poor man. I need to know that you're going to be looking for whoever did it along with the police. It would go a long way towards helping me deal with it right now."

"I'll consider it," I said, not wanting to tell her that I'd already decided to do exactly what she was asking of me. "Can you tell me anything about John Rumsfield or the writers that might help in my investigation, if I decide to do it?"

"I didn't know the publisher any more than you did, but he seemed to take joy in tweaking his authors. I thought there would be a more convivial atmosphere when they were all together, but I overheard something when they were in the green room that makes me wonder about that."

"What did you hear?"

"Alexa Masters was threatening to get out of the second book in her contract, and John was furious with her."

"How could she do that? I just assumed she'd be locked in with the publishing house until the contract ran its course."

"Not if there is a breach on the publisher's part," Paige said.

"What kind of breach?"

"Alexa claimed that John was lowballing her sales figures so he could cheat her later on her royalties. The publisher was absolutely livid when Brad chimed in that he was planning to do an audit himself."

"How did Simon and Bev react to the fight?"

"They both tried to fade into the woodwork. Evidently Brad and Alexa were his rock stars. Simon and Bev just looked happy to have deals in place."

"For however long those might last," I said, without realizing that Paige might not be privy to everything that I was.

"What is that supposed to mean?"

"John was going to drop them both," I admitted. "It gives them both a motive, doesn't it?"

"If I didn't know Brad, I'd think that all four of them had reason to want the man dead."

I studied her hard for a moment before I asked the next question on my mind. "Are you that convinced Brad didn't have anything to do with it?"

"Yes," Paige said simply.

When she didn't say anything else, I asked, "Is there any reason in particular you feel that strongly about it?"

"I don't want to talk about that," she said curtly. Changing the subject, she said, "I understand someone used a bookend to kill him."

"It was one of the geode pairs," I said, hoping that Chief Grant wouldn't mind if I disclosed that fact. Just to be safe, I added, "Don't tell anyone that I just told you that. I'm not sure I was supposed to mention it even to you, okay?"

"I won't say a word. Besides, who would I tell?" she asked me.

I could think of lots of possibilities, but I had a question for her. "Were any nonfiction titles stored in the green room last night?"

"What? No, I'm fairly certain they were not."

"Are you sure about that?"

"I am, unless one was misplaced. Why do you ask?"

I took a deep breath, and before I revealed what I knew, I said, "Paige, this is important. What I'm about to tell you could be critical in figuring this out. If you breathe it to a soul, you could jeopardize lives." Okay, maybe I was being a little melodramatic, but who knew what might arouse a murderer's suspicions? "Can you promise me that you won't tell anyone else what I'm about to tell you?"

"I promise," Paige said solemnly. I didn't have a bible handy for her to swear an oath on, but I felt as though I could trust her. After all, she didn't have a reason to want to see the publisher dead.

As far as I knew, anyway.

"Okay. Evidently John Rumsfield had a few moments of consciousness before he died, and he reached out with his bloodied right hand and grabbed a book off one of the stacks."

"Did one of the authors at the signing write it?" she asked, her face suddenly ashen.

"No, it was written by a man named Hebron Smith."

"I'm not familiar with that name off the bat. What was the title?"

"*Seven Deadly Mushrooms*," I said. "Does that ring any bells?"

"Did you just say 'deadly'?" she asked me, her voice barely above a whisper.

"I did."

"Don't you see? That's Brad's favorite buzzword for his titles. His two best-known books are *A Deadly Kiss* and *A Deadly Embrace*. John Rumsfield was trying to tell us who murdered him."

CHAPTER 9

"IT'S GOT TO BE A coincidence," I said, even though I hated even considering that as a possibility. "The word 'deadly' can't be that unusual in a book title."

"It sounds a little too on the nose to be a coincidence to me," Paige said. "Should we tell the police chief?"

"Let me dig around a little and see what else I can uncover first," I said. I didn't want Paige planting the idea in Chief Grant's head without more reason to think it might be true quite yet.

"So, you'll do it?" she asked, her eyes full of hope. "You'll look into John's murder?"

"I'm not making any promises, but I'll see what I can do," I answered her.

"That's all I can ask. What else can I do to help?"

"Right now, nothing. I need to dig around some, but I'm sure I'll need to ask you more questions later. Do you have any idea how long your bookstore is going to be closed?"

Paige looked as though she wanted to cry. "It might be until tomorrow before I get it back," she said. "There goes my chance of making it a success."

"Don't be too hasty about that," I said. "When you do open back up, your business is going to boom for at least a few weeks, unless I miss my guess."

"Why would you say that? Who in their right mind would want to visit a place where a murder had been so recently committed?"

"Trust me, after it happened in my shop once, I couldn't keep the people away."

"That's kind of macabre, isn't it?"

I shrugged. "My attitude is that you can't care about *why* people are visiting your shop, you just need to be poised to take advantage of it. I know it must sound kind of heartless to you, but it's not like you're planning to promote the murder. If some people are motivated to come in and have a look around, what are you supposed to do about it? I'm not saying you should go out of your way to profit from what happened, but it shouldn't be the reason your bookstore goes under before it even has a chance, either."

"I'm not sure I can bring myself to look at it that way," she said with a hint of uncertainty in her voice.

I could see her point of view, but I was afraid that she might be a little too fragile to get through this if she didn't toughen up. "In the end, you have to do what you think is best. Hey, is the chief waving to you?"

I'd seen Chief Grant over Paige's shoulder motioning to her.

"He is. I wonder what he wants."

"There's only one way to find out, isn't there?" I asked.

I unlocked the front door to let her out, but instead of securing it after her, I decided to tag along and see if I could learn anything new that might be helpful to my cause.

Chief Grant just smiled when he saw me following Paige, and he didn't say a word to me when we reached him, so I had to assume that it was okay with him that I was there.

"What's going on, Chief? Did you find something else?" Paige asked him.

"Not inside, but we found something in the alley out back, and I was wondering if you'd have a look at it."

He held out a single sheet of paper, and I saw that it had been formatted to look like a book, with a header reading WIP and a page number on the bottom. It was number thirty, if that had any meaning to anyone. "Why would I recognize this?"

"I thought it might be a page from one of the writers," he admitted.

"I don't think so," she said as she glanced at it and then handed it back to him.

"How can you be so sure?" Chief Grant asked her.

"From what I've learned, writers don't even submit paper copies of their books anymore. Everything is done electronically, but even if they were going to submit a hardcopy, they wouldn't format it to look like a book."

"So, that's a mistake that an amateur might make, is that what you're saying?" I asked her.

"Yes, I would think so. Why?"

"I know someone who might have lost a sheet from his book," I said, and then I looked at Chief Grant before I added, "Abner Mason."

"I'll talk to him right now," the chief said, and then he thanked us both for our time.

"Any idea how long it will be until I can reopen?" she asked the chief before he could go.

"As soon as possible. I promise. In the meantime, why don't you go home and try to get some rest. I'll personally call you when we're ready to release the bookstore back to you."

"That might be a good idea after all," she said. Turning to me, she took one of my hands in hers and held it tightly. "Thank you, Suzanne."

"Happy to help," I said.

Once she was gone, the police chief looked at me and smiled. "Any reason in particular she'd thank you like that?"

"I gave her some coffee and a donut," I said with a shrug. "Maybe she's just really grateful."

He wasn't buying it, but it wasn't that important to me that he did. "Sure. Let's go with that, shall we? Now I need to go find Abner and ask him about this."

"Want me to tag along?" I asked him playfully.

"Thanks for the offer, but I've got this. Besides, I thought you still had donuts you needed to make."

"That's nearly always the case," I said with a shrug.

"Back to it, then," he said, and then he was gone as well.

I made my way back across the street and let myself into Donut Hearts. He was right. It was indeed time to make the donuts again, but as soon as I closed the shop for the day, I was going to start digging into the publisher's murder.

I just hoped that Grace would be able to take some time off work to help, but if she couldn't, I'd plow on by myself, even if none of my other assistants could do it.

I couldn't just let someone get away with murder.

Not on my watch.

By nine that morning, I'd already told my story to a dozen customers, selling many more donuts than I would have on a normal day. I'd had a hunch that might be the case, so I'd nearly doubled my output. I could only take the advice I'd given Paige. I couldn't make folks come into Donut Hearts, but if they did, for whatever reason, I was going to have something ready to sell them. There was a fascination with murder that I just didn't get, but I knew from experience that if I was reticent in my retelling, people would fill in the gaps with their imaginations, and besides, no one had the brass to come right out and ask me about it without buying at least something, and I made sure to try to upsell every last one of them.

Mayor George Morris came in, looked around at my crowded

shop, and then he said, "Business appears to be booming this morning."

"You know how it is," I said quietly. "Murder brings out people in droves."

"Sad business, that," George answered as he glanced over at the building across the street. It had been empty for so long that I'd almost begun to overlook it, my eyes always going to the Boxcar Grill instead, or even the park. Now it was extremely difficult to ignore.

"I'm surprised you weren't over there earlier." Though he was mayor now, once upon a time George had been a pretty good cop, at least according to some of the stories I'd heard.

"I thought about it, but in the end, I decided to try to give the chief plenty of space," the mayor said after he ordered a cup of coffee and an old-fashioned cake donut. "After all, Phillip has found a way to do it, and I'm trying to follow his example."

"My stepfather isn't interested in *any* crimes that have happened in the past ten years."

"I know," George said with a grin. "He cornered me in the diner last week and couldn't stop talking about a disappearance. I thought it was current until he made a reference to his theory that the supposed victim actually took the train out of town. Those tracks haven't been active in a long time."

I happened to own the rights to the rails themselves, thanks to a dear departed blacksmith who'd become my friend, so I knew what he was talking about. "What can I say? He finds it fascinating."

"And your mother?"

"Momma loves him. That appears to be enough."

"It's more than enough, if you ask me," George said as he took a stool near the counter so we could continue to chat.

"How's your love life going, Mr. Mayor?" I asked him with a grin.

"I'm too busy for that sort of nonsense these days," he replied gruffly.

So, not good then. "If you ask me, it's the best kind of nonsense there is."

"Speaking of love, where's your husband? I haven't seen him around town lately."

"He's out of town," I said, trying to leave as many details out as I could.

"Jake hasn't found himself a job, has he?" George asked.

"No, he's just helping out a friend," I answered.

"Good for him," the mayor said. Glancing back at the bookstore, he asked, "Have you spoken with Paige since you found the publisher's body?"

"Yes, she came by," I said, and then I took another order. At least the woman didn't ask about what we were discussing. I didn't recognize her, and I wondered if she'd stopped in on the spur of the moment. When the mayor referred to me finding a body, she stiffened at the news, and as she scurried out of there, I wondered if she'd ever make a repeat visit.

"Sorry about that," George said once she was gone.

"No worries. I'm more than making up for it with everyone else."

"Now, about Paige. Do you happen to know if she's going to keep the bookstore open?"

"I don't know that she has any choice," I said. "She's sunk nearly her entire inheritance into it."

"Well, I hope she keeps it going. This town has long needed a bookstore, and I'm glad someone finally stepped up and started one," the mayor said.

"As a matter of fact, I was surprised you weren't at the grand opening yesterday cutting a ribbon or something," I remarked as I cleaned away a few dirty dishes.

"I wanted to be there, but I was seeing to something out of town," George said.

"Business or pleasure?" I asked him. I knew that I was being a little rude, but I'd known the man a long time, and there weren't many boundaries between us when it came to topics of conversation.

"If you must know, I had a date in Charlotte, and to top it off, my truck broke down, so I had to spend the night."

"So, the date must have gone really well," I said with a wicked grin.

"I stayed in a hotel. Alone. She was, how can I put this? Odd. Yes, that's the best way to describe her."

"Some of the most interesting people I know are a little odd."

"'Odd' isn't the right word, then. Strange. She told me that she didn't believe in government, including mayors or police officers, both of which I have served as in our community."

"What *does* she believe in, then?"

"Anarchy, as far as I could tell; total and complete anarchy. My friend who fixed us up didn't tell me any of that, of course. I think he was getting me back for something, though I can't for the life of me come up with something that I might have done to him to deserve that. Fortunately, I found somebody to fix my truck this morning, and I just got back in town ten minutes before I walked over here."

"How'd you hear about the murder so quickly, then?"

"You're kidding, right? I took one step into my office, and I was suddenly inundated with people asking me if we were living in the murder capital of the South."

"We haven't had *that* many, have we?"

"I don't know, but the ones we do get seem to be flashier than the norm. I don't think the body count is much higher than any other city our size; it's just that they seem to be a little too memorable. Anyway, I've got to get to work easing some fears around town." George paused and leaned forward before telling me softly, "If you need me, I'm here for you."

"In what capacity?" I asked him.

"You know darn well what I'm talking about. You found the body. There's no way in the world you're not going to dig into this, with or without Chief Grant's permission."

"I might do a little snooping," I admitted.

"That a girl. You know where to find me if you need me."

"I appreciate that."

"Hang on a second. Jake is out of town. That means that Grace is going to help you, right? You shouldn't fly solo on this, Suzanne. If she can't help, I'm sure your mother and stepfather would pitch in, or I could even take a few days off myself. It would be like it used to be."

"I'll let you know, but thanks for the offer," I said. I was reluctant to use George for any of my investigations any more, since I'd gotten him shot helping me once a long time ago. His limp had vanished almost completely, but I still felt guilty about putting him in harm's way, even though it seemed as though it had all happened a lifetime ago.

"You do that," he said.

CHAPTER 10

I T WAS NEARING CLOSING TIME at eleven and I still hadn't heard from Grace, though I'd called her at nine that morning. My call had gone straight to voicemail, and I had to wonder if she wasn't tied up with something work related. Her job as a supervisor for a large beauty product company gave her a great deal of leeway sometimes and none at all at others. I'd have to call her after Emma and I closed the shop for the day, and if I still couldn't get hold of her, I'd take the mayor's advice and ask Momma and Phillip for their help with the case. I'd worked with them both in the past, but if I had my druthers, it would be Grace or Jake working on the investigation with me. Momma seemed to still see me as her baby girl, while Phillip tended to want whatever my mother wanted, which was for me to be safe. I could understand the sentiment, but it could really impede my investigations.

I was just about to lock the front door when Grace hurried in. "Whew. I made it just in time," she said, nearly out of breath.

"Did you run all the way over here from your place?" I asked her as I shut and locked the door behind her.

"No, but I had to rush to wrap things up for the day. Sorry I didn't call you back, but I had my hands full."

"Grace, you don't have to drop what you're doing to help me whenever I call."

"Suzanne, I live for these moments. As a matter of fact, I've worked things out where my schedule is clear for the next two days. All I have to do is plow some paperwork at night, and I'm all yours."

"Excellent," I said with relief. "The truth is, I'm happy to have you."

"So, how should we get started?"

"Well, Emma and I need ten or fifteen minutes to wrap things up here before we do anything else. While you're waiting, you have two choices. You can pitch in, or just grab a coffee and a donut and let us get our work done."

"How about door number three?" she asked. "I could make some phone calls while I'm waiting."

"About the case?"

"No, it's just a few loose ends I'd like to tie up with my job."

I frowned at her. "Are you *sure* I'm not putting you in a bind?"

"I'm positive," she answered, "though I will take that coffee, if you don't mind. I figure it's so close to lunch time I'd better skip the treat, since we'll probably be grabbing a bite a little later."

"Coffee coming right up," I said. After I served her, I got busy on my end of our closing routine.

A little later, Emma came out from the kitchen, said hello to Grace, and then she turned to me and said, "There are three dozen donuts left, which, considering how many you made, isn't all that bad. What should we do with them?"

"Why don't you box them up? I might be able to use them today myself, if you don't mind."

"Why should I mind?" she asked me.

"I know you like taking them to class with you," I replied.

"Classes are cancelled today," she said with a smile. "A water main broke on campus, so I got a text not to show up."

"Wow, it's nice of them to let you know so quickly."

"They started the texting chain as a way of telling us about any impending dangers on campus, but it's kind of evolved into a general forum now."

"So, what are you going to do with a free afternoon?" I asked her as she boxed the donuts in question.

"I called Barton, and he's going to slip away a few hours," she said with a grin.

"How romantic," Grace said from her table.

Emma shrugged. "Our schedules are so crazy, we have to make time for each other whenever we can, or we'd never see each other."

"You can take off now, if you'd like," I offered. "I'll finish whatever needs to be done in back."

"Thanks, but I've got time."

After Emma was gone, Grace asked me, "Why the sudden urge for extra donuts?"

"I thought we might use them as bribes to get folks to talk to us if we need any persuaders," I admitted.

"Excellent. It's just like the good old days," she said with approval. "Any chance we can assume secret identities as well?" It wasn't that crazy a question, since we'd done it more than once in the past in the course of one of our investigations.

"Sorry. Everybody involved in this case already knows who I am."

"Oh, well. Maybe next time," Grace said and then took another sip of coffee.

"I don't know about you, but I sincerely hope that there *is* no next time."

"You realize that you say that every time, don't you?" Grace asked me.

"Who knows? Maybe one day it will actually be true."

To my delight, everything balanced in the register, and we were ready to go in no time. "Should I drive?" I asked her. "I know how you feel about the smell of donuts in your car."

"That depends. Are you going to go home and shower before we start investigating?"

I smelled my arm. "I don't smell, do I?"

"Your nose has gone deaf to the smell of donuts, hasn't it?"

"I'm not sure that a nose can go deaf, but yes, you're probably right. I can go clean up if you want me to."

"Don't do it on my account," she said. "Besides, I like it, and we're going to be hauling around three dozen donuts to boot anyway, so why not?"

"So then, I'm driving," I said with a grin.

"If you wouldn't mind."

"I'd be delighted." We put the boxes in the back of my Jeep, and then we headed out.

"Who should we speak with first?" Grace asked me once we were on our way.

"I think it would make sense to go to the Bentley Hotel in Union Square, since that's where the authors are all staying." I'd overheard that last night, and I'd filed the information away in case I might need it. It was amazing what was useless one day was so valuable the next. Maybe that was why I had a hard time ever throwing anything out.

"Was the publisher checked in there, too? I wouldn't mind having a look around his room," Grace said.

"I'm not sure where he was staying, but I doubt that we can just walk in and check it out."

"It's a real pity everyone doesn't just give us a free pass to do whatever we wanted to, isn't it?" Grace asked me with a grin. "It would make our investigations so much easier. Maybe we can use one of those boxes of donuts as a bribe for someone in housekeeping."

"We'll have to wait and see what happens," I said as I drove to Union Square. The Bentley Hotel was nice, an independent place that had never been part of a chain, and it had an older elegance about it that I liked. I'd never stayed there myself, since I lived just one town away, but I'd eaten there with Momma a few times over the years, always on special occasions.

"Should we eat at the restaurant, since we'll already be there, or should we go to Napoli's while we're in town?" Grace asked. Food was always a priority for us when we were together, whether we were investigating a murder or not.

"I love the DeAngelis women and their food more than anybody, but it just makes sense to grab a bite while we're at the hotel, doesn't it?"

"I won't tell them if you won't," Grace said with a grin.

"It's not like we're cheating on them."

"Maybe a little, but I can live with the guilt if you can," she said. "So, while we're driving, how about giving me a recap of what you know so far? You've had quite a lot longer to think about this case than I have. Start with what you saw last night when you found the body. You should have called me, by the way. I could have been there for you."

"I never really had the chance, and by the time I was back at Donut Hearts, I just wanted to put it all out of my mind," I said.

"Apology accepted," Grace said with a smile.

"Funny, but I don't remember apologizing."

"It was implied, though," she replied.

"I suppose it was at that. Okay, here goes. I was going to work this morning when I noticed that the bookstore's front door was open. I parked the Jeep in my usual spot and decided to investigate."

"Without calling the police first? That was awfully daring of you, wasn't it?"

"I called them, but Glenda was handling the phone, and we were having trouble connecting. Anyway, I was going to wait outside when I could swear I heard something in the bookstore. I couldn't wait for Henry to show up, so I went in, flipping the lights on along the way. I didn't see anything out of the ordinary until I got to the break room. The lights wouldn't turn on, but fortunately I had my heavy-duty flashlight with me. That's when I found John Rumsfield's body lying on the floor with the geode bookend nearby, bloodied from the assault." I shivered a little upon reliving it, remembering the scene a little too vividly for my taste. "There was a book near his right hand, and it had a smear of blood on it from his index finger. Hang on a second. I took some shots with my phone before the chief showed up. Old habits die hard."

I handed my phone to her, and after she studied the photos, Grace said, "Please tell me this book was written by one of our suspects."

"If that were the case, we'd hardly need to be digging into this, would we? Though Paige has a theory about that as well."

"I'd love to hear what it is. What book was it, anyway? The image isn't all that great."

"Sorry, but my hands were shaking a little, what with me just finding a dead body and all," I said.

"I apologize," Grace said seriously. "That was out of line, even for me. What was the title?"

"*Seven Deadly Mushrooms*," I said.

Before I could explain Paige's theory, Grace whistled softly. "And Brad Winslow's two bestselling books are *A Deadly Kiss* and *A Deadly Embrace*. She thinks he did it, doesn't she?"

"I think it's a stretch myself, but yes, that's what she thinks. It's all a little too coincidental for my taste."

"Or it could be an attempt to frame him for the murder," Grace said.

"What do you mean?"

"Suzanne, we're dealing with mystery and suspense writers.

I think we should expect to find things that are overly dramatic and imaginative. After all, that's how they make their livings."

"It's a possibility, isn't it?" I asked, having a hard time grasping someone actually doing that in real life.

"I'd say it's more like a probability. I'm not sure how much of a chance there is that it's exactly what it looks like, but I doubt that it's very good."

"We can't ignore the obvious, either," I reminded her. "Remember. Hoofbeats are usually horses."

"But sometimes they do come from zebras," she said.

"We'll keep our eyes open to all of the possibilities," I agreed.

"I can live with that. Now tell me about the people we'll be speaking with today. Is there anyone *besides* the authors we saw on the panel last night?"

"Well, there's Abner Mason," I said.

"I have a hard time imagining Abner killing anyone, especially a stranger."

"Grace, he's obsessed with getting his book published, and the chief found a page from his manuscript behind the bookstore. At the very least, we need to ask him some questions about what he did last night and who he spoke with."

"We can track him down after we get back into town," Grace said. "What do you know about the authors involved? Have you learned anything since last night?"

"Brad Winslow was leaving the publishing house—that was what the big announcement was about he mentioned before he walked out—and Rumsfield wasn't happy about letting him go. I could easily see them having another argument that escalated into murder. Then again, Simon Gant and Bev Worthington were both being dropped, and to a writer, that might seem like the end of the world to them. In desperate times, who knows how someone will react?"

"That leaves Alexa Masters. Did she have a beef with the publisher?"

"There's a rumor going around that Rumsfield was low-balling her sales figures so he could cheat her out of some of her royalties."

"Wow, he was a real prince, wasn't he? Okay, we've got a solid game plan. We'll keep talking to all of them until we get one of them to confess," she said with a laugh. "Suzanne, I'm kind of surprised Paige Hill isn't on your list."

The suggestion surprised me. "Why would she be? What animosity could she possibly have against the publisher?"

"I don't know, but she admits to having had a relationship with Brad Winslow, and she *was* involved in every aspect of the festivities last night. Not only that, but she was the one who pointed out that the word 'deadly' appeared in both the book found by Rumsfield's body and in Winslow's titles. Maybe she did it to frame her estranged boyfriend, and she was afraid no one would see it, so she pointed it out herself."

"Do you honestly think that Paige is that imaginative?"

"I don't see why not. After all, she opened a bookstore, so you'd have to believe that she's passionate about reading, and don't forget, over half that store is stocked with mysteries, so I'm guessing she's a big fan of the genre. Yes, I can see her doing it."

"Okay then, we'll keep her on our list as well."

We were at the Bentley quicker than I expected. Our conversation had been so gripping that I hadn't noticed the miles flying past as I drove.

It was time to start interviewing our suspects.

I just hoped they were willing to speak with us.

CHAPTER 11

"**I**sn't that Brad Winslow sitting over there alone?" Grace asked me as we walked into the lobby of the hotel. I glanced over and saw that it was indeed Brad, hunched over a notebook and staring at it intently. After jotting something down, he stared off into space for a moment, slammed the cover closed, and then he stood up with a scowl.

"Is there something wrong?" I asked him.

Our presence, as well as my question, clearly caught him off guard. "You look familiar. Do I know you? You're not a crazy fan stalking me, are you?"

In your dreams, I wanted to say, but I refrained. "I was at the signing last night, but you left before I could get you to sign a book for me," I said.

Flipping the notebook open again to the back, he scrawled something, ripped the sheet out, and then he handed it to me. "Thanks for reading my work."

"Actually, I've never read anything you've written," I said.

Grace started to laugh, but then she managed to suppress it before Brad could catch on.

"Oh, you're one of those," he said in obvious disdain.

"One of what?" I asked him.

"A fame seeker. Sorry, but I'm not interested. You're a little old for my tastes."

Was he actually suggesting what I thought he was suggesting? It was time to clear the air. "Paige Hill asked us to look into what happened to John Rumsfield last night. You remember Paige, don't you? She told us all about you, so I wouldn't bother trying to deny it."

"Why would I deny it?" He looked at us both carefully, and then he sniffed my hair. "I smell donuts on you."

"That's because I make them for a living," I said, wondering if I should have taken Grace's advice about grabbing a quick shower before we got started.

"Then I take it your investigation isn't sanctioned by the police," he replied.

"We've had some luck in the past solving a murder or two on our own," I admitted. "Honestly, I would think that you'd do everything you could to help someone solve your publisher's murder, since you seem to be a logical chief suspect."

The writer looked surprised by my comment. "Why on earth would you say something like that?"

"You didn't see me, but I witnessed you arguing with your publisher yesterday in front of the bookstore, which happens to be across the street from my donut shop. There was a great deal of bad blood there, so you have no reason to bother denying it. It was pretty obvious even from across the street."

"Big deal. John was unhappy with me. I personally was thrilled with the situation."

That was an odd statement to make. "You were going to break your contract, weren't you? That was why you were having a press conference in Charlotte. You were going to announce it."

"Big deal," he said smugly. "I was planning to move to a larger publisher for my next two books. Obviously John didn't want to lose me, but there was nothing he could do about it, no matter what he might have thought. I happen to have a get-out-of-jail-free card."

"So, you were still under contract with him," I said, picking up on his lead.

"Contracts can be broken by either party, given cause."

"And exactly what cause did you have?" Grace asked.

"I'm not about to tell you. Are you a baker, too? Surely not, based on the look of you."

"I happen to work for a cosmetics company," she replied.

"Another sound basis for detecting. If you two are set on finding a killer, which I highly doubt is possible, I'd suggest you speak with Alexa Masters."

"Why her?" I asked.

"She is the one who threatened John Rumsfield if he didn't release her from her contract. You see, she found out he was cheating her, but the bad thing is, there is absolutely nothing she can do about it. You wouldn't believe how one-sided the contract she signed is, all in John's favor. She didn't even have the right to audit the accounts of the publisher! It was criminal, if you ask me. He took advantage of her, and I don't doubt she wanted out. She just doesn't know what I do."

"And what's that?" Grace pressed him.

"What harm would it do to tell you now? John started Starboard House after leaving one of the big publishers. He took great pride in entering into his agreements as an individual and not as a corporation. That left him too vulnerable to lawsuits though, so he sent out a letter last week stating that most of the contracts he'd signed were cancelled, and if any author wanted to be considered for further publication, they had to sign a waiver not to sue him as an individual."

"That's a crazy way to run a business," Grace said.

"Yes, he set it up that way against the advice of his attorneys. He thought it gave him an edge signing fresh talent, but instead, it merely saddled him with a different set of liabilities. The main point right now, though, is that with his death, *all* of the contracts automatically become null and void, according to an attorney I consulted about the matter a few weeks ago."

"That doesn't make you look exactly innocent," I told him.

"Nonsense. I was leaving anyway, he was dumping Simon and Bev, and the rest of his stable doesn't amount to much at all. We were his all-stars, you see. That leaves only Alexa who stands to gain from his demise."

"Wouldn't the fact that he was dumping Bev and Simon give them motives as well?"

He nodded. "Yes, I considered that possibility as well. It's credible, but I still think Alexa did it."

"You seem to have given this a great deal of thought in a short amount of time," I said.

"But don't you see? That's what I do for a living. I imagine situations and I project the ramifications of their occurrences. There are a few things you should know about fiction writers. First of all, we lie for a living. Second, we're professional assassins, getting paid to murder people, in fiction if not in real life, and lastly, we see levels and subtleties beyond what the ordinary person might notice. If one of us did kill John, you'll never discover who did it. You aren't dealing with a typical criminal here. This act was committed by someone with the ability to play the game on many different levels."

I wasn't about to let him grandstand like that without challenge. "First of all, it's clear that the murder wasn't planned. He was hit with a bookend found two feet from the body. Does that scream premeditation to you?" I asked him.

"On the surface, no. Then again, maybe it was staged to appear that way."

"You seem to have a pretty high opinion of your fellow authors, at least of their talents at planning out murder," Grace said.

"For the most part, we are all intricate planners, plotting out our stories long before we record a single word."

I protested, "My book club has learned that just as many of you plot as you go by the seat of your pants, though."

"True, there are some of that ilk out there, but it's the sign of lesser ability, at least in my opinion."

"I wonder how they feel about you?" Grace asked.

"They think plotters are so rigid they can't change the story along the way, even if a better idea comes along," he said.

Elizabeth had read several articles about plotters versus pantsers, and she'd shared them with us in book club. The camps were as separate as could be, from what she'd relayed to us, and I was beginning to suspect that she'd been right.

"Is it true?"

"No, it's utter rubbish," he said. "Now if you'll excuse me, I must walk."

"What an odd thing to say," Grace said.

"Not really. Walking allows me to think. I'm stuck on a particularly difficult part of the outline for my next book, so I have to go." He headed for the door, but before he left, he turned back to us and said, "A word of warning. We might seem harmless to you, sitting alone and jotting down our fantastic tales, but let me remind you that someone killed John Rumsfield in a very concrete way."

"That sounds kind of like a threat to me," Grace said to me. "How about you?"

"I suppose that it could be construed as one," I answered. "That makes him sound a little guilty, doesn't it?"

"I suppose it does," she answered.

Brad Winslow looked at us both with contempt, and then he left the lobby.

"That's one odd bird, isn't it?" a woman's voice said behind us coming from the restaurant entrance.

"Bev. It's so nice to see you," I said.

"I didn't mean to eavesdrop," she started, and then she

stopped herself. "That's a big fat lie. I love listening in on other conversations. Sometimes I get my best sparks from them. So, Brad claimed he was getting away scot-free from his contract. That's not what I heard."

"What did you hear?" I asked her.

"Evidently he was dating a woman from the accounting department for the strict purpose of accessing information about how John did business. She told him that Rumsfield routinely stole royalties from his authors, and Brad was going to use it to try to get out of his contract."

"How did you hear that?" I asked her.

"I overheard the two men shouting about it last night after the signing," she said. "Simon had a headache, so he came back here to rest, but I wanted to walk the streets and take some photos to get the feel of this town. I may very well set my next series in a place like this, and I wanted a record of it. Anyway, I was sitting in the park admiring the night when I heard them arguing. John pressed Brad about his announcement, and when Brad told him what he was going to do, and more importantly why, John just laughed at him. It was one of the most wicked, cruel laughs I've ever heard in my life."

"Wasn't he worried about his theft of royalties coming to light?" Grace asked her.

"He claimed that he wasn't. He told Brad that the accountant changed her tune when she found out Brad was dating a B-list actress at the same time he was wooing her. John told him that he had her assurance that she would say nothing to support Brad and that if he spoke one word against his publisher, he'd see him in court. John would do it, too. He once sued an author for not allowing him first refusal on his next work, and what's more, he won the case. Poor Milford was nearly bankrupted by the verdict, and what was worse, no other publisher would touch him. The terms of the verdict didn't even allow him to self-publish his work. That's what I'm going to do. I'm quite tired of Fanny, anyway. My next sleuth is going to be quite a bit slinkier, and more stylish, too. I have big plans. You see, John's murder doesn't have any impact on me at all. I was secretly hoping he'd dump me, anyway, even though he'd keep the rights to Fanny tied up forever. What an evil contract that man used against us. Poor Simon isn't so sure what he's going to do next, but he'll come around."

"Are you two close?" I asked her softly.

"Where did you hear that?" Bev asked with a snap in her voice that hadn't been there before.

"Is it true?" Grace asked her.

"My relationship with Simon Gant is no one else's business," she said. "Now, if you'll excuse me, I need to get a bite to eat."

I wasn't done speaking with her yet. "Do you mind if we join you?"

Bev looked as though she'd rather chew glass, but she simply shrugged. "It's a free country."

We all walked into the dining room together. Simon was already there, and when he saw Bev, his face lit up. That went away the moment he realized we were walking into the restaurant with her. He might not have known what we were up to, but he was surely unhappy about sharing Bev with anyone else.

Simon stood as the three of us joined him at his table, but before he could say a word, Bev spoke. "These women are investigating John's murder, Simon. Be careful what you say."

"Are you with the police?" Simon asked us, looking at us each in turn carefully.

"We're more freelance than official," I said. "Do you mind if we join you?"

Instead of answering, Simon looked at Bev, who shrugged. "I suppose it's all right," he said.

We all got the buffet, which worked out for us, since Grace

and I had planned to eat there anyway. It was a bit pricy for my budget, but I really couldn't slip out and grab a burger somewhere else. This was one of those times when I had to just grin and bear it, though I might be eating stale donuts for a while.

We were just beginning to eat our lunches when Bev got a phone call. From the expression on her face, it wasn't particularly good news. "If you'll excuse me, I need to take this."

She walked out into the lobby, and I thought about following her out to see what was going on, but I doubted that would work with Simon right there.

Grace asked softly, "You really care for her, don't you?"

Simon was clearly caught by surprise by the question, and he didn't answer it directly. "John was going to dump us both. I've already got another deal lined up with a smaller publisher, but she's going to go it on her own. I worry that she won't be able to make it. I'm afraid losing her deal with Starboard House was quite a blow."

"Enough to give her motive for murder?" I asked him.

"What? Of course not. Bev wouldn't hurt a fly."

"Not even if that fly was about to endanger her income, as well as her way of life?" Grace asked.

"Not even then. She and I don't have enough at stake to do something so dramatic, anyway. If I were writing this, I'd look hard at Brad Winslow. He had the most to lose, even more than Alexa."

"You don't like him very much, do you?" I asked, remembering their argument the day before.

"He's an arrogant blowhole who believes self-promotion is more important than actual work," Simon said. "I loathe him. If it had been his body found in the bookstore, I would expect to be near the top of the police's list of suspects, but I had no reason to kill John."

"Other than him dropping you, you mean," I reminded him.

"Like I said, it's not enough of a motive for murder," he said, brushing off my jibe.

"You could have thought you were killing Brad instead of John, though," Grace said. "They had a similar build, and if the room was dark, it could have been a mistake."

I knew that chances were pretty good that John had been facing his killer when he'd been struck down, but the real question was, did Simon know that? Grace was trying to trap him, and I found myself admiring her even more for it.

"Was he killed from behind? He must have been, since the two men looked nothing alike from the front. Interesting," Simon said, looking confused. "I understand some kind of blunt object was used, is that correct?"

"I'm not entirely positive about that," I said, lying myself.

"Well, if he was struck from behind, then mistaken identity might be an avenue to investigate. If not, then it's just plain old murder."

"I'm curious about something. If you were plotting this as a book, how would you have done it so that you could get away with it?" I asked him.

I wasn't sure what his reaction might be, but his laugh surprised me. "That's the thing. I wouldn't plot it at all."

"Because it's too mundane, or is it just too hard to believe?" I asked.

"I don't believe in tying myself down to a rigid format like some of my contemporaries," Simon said as Bev walked back into the room. She didn't look particularly pleased as she took her place at the table again. I took the opportunity to grab a bite of the meatloaf I'd gotten. It was good, but Momma's was better, hands down.

"Are you okay?" Simon asked her rather solicitously.

"That was the police chief. He wants to speak with us both, and what's more, he'll be here in ten minutes."

"Why am I not surprised?" Simon asked. "Of course he'd look at us. Don't worry, my dear. We'll be fine," he said as he patted her hand.

Bev allowed it for a moment until she realized that we were watching them. Quickly pulling her hand away, she said, "I'm sure you're right."

I was about to say something when Grace kneed me. When I glanced over at her, she shot her glance to the door. I could see Alexa Masters speaking with the clerk at the front desk, and I knew what she had in mind.

"If you'll excuse us, we need to go," Grace said.

"What about your bill?" Simon asked. "We're not buying you lunch."

Before I could reach for my wallet, Grace threw two twenties down on the table. "That will more than cover it. I'm sure we'll be speaking again soon."

"I wouldn't count on it," Bev said, clearly hoping that she was finished with us once and for all. She should be so lucky.

"Let me pay you back," I said as we made our way out of the restaurant and into the lobby.

"Can we talk about it later?" she asked as we approached Alexa. "We have work to do."

"Fine," I said.

Grace and I stood just behind the author, and I couldn't help listening in to her conversation. "I'm telling you, I need another room. The people next door keep fighting, and I can't get any work done. I must have quiet! Do you have any idea how hard it is to come up with a fresh plot you can't smell from a mile away? I've got to top my first try, and I have no idea how to do it!"

"I'm afraid we don't have any vacancies, ma'am," the clerk told her apologetically. Clearly he wasn't used to getting such passionate pleas from guests.

"Then move someone!"

"Let me see what I can do," the man said, blanching under the assault.

"Alexa, do you have a second?" I asked her as she turned toward us.

"Brad warned me that you two were investigating John's murder," she said with a frown. "He told me that I'd be a fool to talk to you."

"You can't let him stop you," Grace said.

"Are you kidding? That just made me want to talk to you more. Let's go outside, though. It's too stuffy in here. I can't breathe, let alone think."

As we walked outside, I asked, "Are you having trouble with your second book?"

"Is it that obvious? I had all the time I needed to write the first one, but now I have to deliver the next in six months. Six months! It took me longer than that to plot out the first one, and another sixteen months to write it. I'm a slow writer, and what's more, John knew it. Why I ever signed that contract is beyond me."

"So then, his death gives you an out, doesn't it?" Grace asked.

Alexa stopped in her tracks. "Do you honestly believe that I'd murder the man just to escape a book deadline? What kind of monster do you think I am?"

"If you felt trapped, it might be possible though, wouldn't it?" I asked, trying to soften her ire.

"Wouldn't you feel cornered? Imagine having an impossible deadline, and knowing that if you failed to meet it, you could lose everything you worked so long and so hard for. How would you feel?"

"I'd be mad enough to kill somebody," Grace said.

Alexa's head swiveled around violently toward her. "That's ridiculous."

I had to take the heat off Grace. "Okay, if you didn't do it, tell us, how would you go about it?"

"I don't know. The murder in my book was a little too intricate for real life."

"Forgive me, but I haven't had a chance to read it yet," I said. "How did you kill your victim?" It was an odd question, and I hoped no one was walking by who might overhear it. Taken out of context, it could raise quite a few questions in someone's mind.

"I used skin cream laced with poison that would interact only with a certain rare soap that the victim used. It was rather clever, actually. There were six people living in the house at the time, but only one of them was ever in real danger, as long as they stuck to their habits and patterns. We're all just bundles of behaviors, you know."

"I'm afraid John Rumsfield's murder was not nearly as ingenious as that," I said.

"Blunt force trauma. I heard." She looked at me carefully for a moment. "You're the donut maker, aren't you? You discovered the body."

"Guilty on both counts," I said.

Instead of being horrified, she looked delighted, if only for a moment. "You must tell me all about it. You see, I've never actually seen a dead body before."

"I'm not supposed to talk about it," I told her, surprised by the intensity of her interest.

"I completely understand. Was there much blood? Was he disfigured by the blow? How much force would you say it took to do him in?"

"Again, the police have asked me for my discretion," I said.

"Fine," she replied, losing interest in me for the moment.

"Do you have any idea who might have done it?" Grace asked her.

"I'm sure you're speaking with all of my fellow panelists," she said. "Other than that, I suppose Paige Hill, the bookstore owner, might be a suspect due to her proximity. The only other person it might be is that odd man with his homemade book."

"What book is that?" I asked.

"The manuscript, I should have said. Precision of language is important, you know."

I didn't remember signing up for the lecture on language. "What happened?"

"After the signing, I saw a rough-looking brute approach John out in back of the bookstore when he was grabbing a smoke. He had in his hands what must have been a manuscript. I'm guessing he wanted John to read it and give him a critique on the spot. He got that, and more."

"What happened?"

"John read the first page and then flung the entire thing back at him. He said some fairly insulting things, and I thought the man might actually attack him! After a moment though, he gathered the pages up and just slunk away. John laughed at his discomfort, and I thought he was going to regret doing that, but the man just kept going. I tried to tell the police what I'd seen as soon as I heard what happened, but there is a Chief Grant coming out here to interview us all in a few minutes." She looked over our shoulders and frowned. "In fact, unless I miss my guess, that must be the man himself."

CHAPTER 12

T
o no one's surprise, Chief Grant was not particularly pleased upon finding us interviewing one of his suspects. When he discovered that we'd spoken with all of them already, I knew that he'd be unhappier still.

"Suzanne. Grace," he said perfunctorily.

"Don't mind us. We were just leaving," I said.

"I would expect nothing less," he replied. "Miss Masters, thank you for calling. I'm sorry I couldn't get here sooner."

She looked a little flustered upon seeing the chief, and I wasn't the only one to notice her quick smile. "It's quite all right. Shall we go up to my room where we can have some privacy?"

"Of course," the chief said, and then added, "Ladies, I'll speak with you both soon."

"You bet you will," Grace said with an artificial lilt to her words that made me think our police chief was in for a whole lot of hurt later.

"Did you see that? Can you believe it?" she asked me after they were gone. "That woman was practically salivating over Stephen."

"He's a good-looking guy," I said. "What did you expect?"

Grace looked at me long and hard before she spoke. "You're not taking *her* side, are you?"

I knew better than to do anything as foolish and reckless as that. "You know that you have nothing to worry about. Stephen Grant is crazy about you."

"I understand that," she said reluctantly. "I still don't have to like it though, do I?"

"No, ma'am. You don't have anything to explain to me. Now, should we hang around here and wait for him to finish up with everyone so we can have another crack at them, or should we head back to April Springs and speak with Abner Mason before your boyfriend gets to him?"

"That shouldn't even be an issue. If I know Stephen, he's already spoken with him," Grace said.

"Then that gives us all the more reason to go back home," I replied.

"Sure, why not? I suppose we've done all of the damage that we can here."

"For now, anyway," I said. "I'd like to speak with them all again, but not until I have more to go on. Let's go see what Abner has to say about the confrontation Alexa witnessed last night."

"If it really was an argument at all," Grace said as we got back into my Jeep and headed to April Springs.

"What do you mean by that? Do you think she made it all up?"

"Not entirely, but you heard Brad. They all lie. I'm perfectly willing to believe that Alexa saw something last night, but I doubt it was a blow-by-blow account. If Rumsfield had done that to Abner, can you imagine for one second that the mechanic would just slink away, given how he feels about his book?"

"No, he probably would have strangled him on the spot," I said.

"Maybe, maybe not, but I certainly can't see him sneaking back into the bookstore later after hours to clobber him then," Grace said.

"So where does that leave us?" I asked her.

"We should go ahead and talk to Abner anyway, and then we see if we can make heads or tails of this mess," Grace said.

It was as good an idea as any, and as we drove back home, we spun out a dozen different scenarios about what *might* have really happened to the book publisher, but by the time we reached the town limits, we were still no closer to solving the man's murder than we'd been when we'd left Union Square. At least I knew where to find our suspect.

"Abner, do you have a minute?" Grace and I asked as we got to the garage where he worked. I was honestly a little surprised to see him still working this late, but it had been worth a try to check, and the hunch had paid off.

"Is the Jeep giving you problems again?" he asked in an open and friendly manner as he wiped his hands on a rag.

"No, it's about the murder last night at the bookstore."

"I don't know anything about that," Abner said, suddenly chilling to us both.

"Has the chief spoken with you yet?" Grace asked.

"That's why I'm working when I should be home microwaving my dinner," the mechanic said. "They find one little piece of paper of mine, and all of a sudden I'm public enemy number one."

"There's a little more to it than that, and you know it," I said.

Abner reached into his back pocket absently and pulled out a large crescent wrench. As he stood there, he began slapping the heavy tool in the palm of his hand. I wasn't sure if he was doing it subconsciously or if it was an attempt to intimidate us. If it was the latter, it was working, at least a little. "So what? I had a conversation with the guy. Why wouldn't I? He could publish my book. I would have been a fool to miss the chance to pitch him."

"And what did he say?"

"He told me that he'd like to look at it, but he wasn't buying any new inventory just now. It was friendly enough."

I had to confront him with what Alexa had told us, but I wasn't all that happy about it, especially with the weighty tool in his hand. "That's odd. We heard that you two had an argument and that John Rumsfield threw your manuscript back in your face as he laughed at you. That doesn't sound very friendly to me."

I glanced over at Grace, and she nodded in support. It had been the right thing to do, confronting the mechanic with what we'd heard, despite how squeamish I was feeling at the moment. It would be fine.

At least I hoped so, anyway.

"So, someone was watching us. Big deal. I've been rejected before, and I'm sure it will happen again. Do you know how many times that lady who wrote *Larry* got turned down? I can take it. I'm a grown man."

"But you did have an argument with John Rumsfield. Are you willing to at least admit that?" I asked him.

"That depends on what you call an argument. Like I said, it was a discussion. That's it."

"When was the last time you saw him, Abner?" Grace asked him.

"When do you think? It was when we talked," Abner insisted. "Sure, he tossed some pages back at me, and I was plenty steamed about it for a second, but after I gathered the book back together, I decided he wasn't worth it."

"What did you do next?" Grace asked him.

"I went home, had a few beers, and then I went to bed. My days start early around here."

"Not as early as mine does," I said with a smile, trying to ease the tension between us a little.

It didn't work.

"Yeah. Whatever. Listen, I didn't kill him, okay? I'm not the scheming type, you know? I thought about punching him on the snout when he laughed at me, but it was just for a second. I decided he probably had better lawyers than I could afford, so I decided to forget about him altogether. Don't you worry, though. I'll see that book published someday, one way or the other."

"I'm sure you will," I said, not believing it for a second. "Did John Rumsfield happen to say anything to you that *wasn't* about your book?" I'd asked him the question on a whim, but sometimes my gut knew best.

"Yeah. He said he couldn't stick around and jabber any more with me. He said that he had a meeting with a *real* writer."

"Did he happen to say who it was?" I asked him.

"No, that was all that he said," Abner replied.

"Do you happen to know where he went after he left you?"

"He went back into the bookstore, but through the back door instead of the front way in," Abner said.

"Wasn't it locked by then?" I asked him.

"If it was, he must have had a key, because he walked into the place like he held the lease on it. Listen, I didn't touch the man, let alone kill him. Now can I please get back to work?"

"It's fine by us," I said, realizing that we'd probably gotten all we were going to out of the man, at least for now. "Thanks for your time."

He pulled out a notebook and jotted something down, which piqued my curiosity. "What did you just write down, Abner?"

The mechanic just smiled at me. "Wouldn't you like to know?"

"What do you think, Suzanne? Was Abner telling the truth?"

I shrugged. "I'm not sure why, but I believe him. He could easily have hit John on the spot, but I can't see him sneaking back and clobbering him with a bookend, can you?"

"I try not to judge what people will or will not do, but I'm inclined to agree with you. If Rumsfield had gotten a black eye, or even a bloody nose, Abner could have done it, but I see him using his hands, not some nearby blunt instrument."

"Unless it was a wrench," I said, remembering the sound of the metal hitting his palm.

"Yeah, maybe that, too," Grace said. "We haven't been able to eliminate a single suspect, have we? Sometimes I think all we do is spin our wheels in the sand."

"You know how this works better than anybody. All we can do for now is collect the pieces of the puzzle and try to fit them together in a way that makes sense."

"This time it's different, though, isn't it?" Grace asked as we drove away.

"How so?"

"Brad Winslow said it himself. Everyone we spoke with, with the single exception of Abner, is a professional liar. They literally earn their livings making things up. Can we really trust *any* of them?"

"I'm a firm believer that even a lie can start with a seed of the truth," I said.

"Wow, that sounds absolutely like some kind of Eastern philosophy," Grace said. "Where did you get that?"

"I may have read it on a soda can once," I admitted, "but that doesn't make it any less valid." I felt my stomach rumble a little. "I don't know about you, but I didn't get much to eat at the restaurant. Are you hungry?"

"I could eat," Grace said with a grin.

"Shall we cook or just go to the diner?" I asked as we got close to the Boxcar Grill, as well as both our homes.

"Do you even have to ask? I'd kill for a hamburger."

"Maybe not the best choice of words, but I agree with the sentiment," I said.

"Yeah, I really should learn to choose my words a little more carefully," she said as I pulled into the parking lot.

Trish was standing at the register when we got there, and there was a look of concern on her face as she spied us. "Just the two women I was looking for," she said in an earnest voice.

"Why? What's going on?"

"You really should talk to your friend. She's having more than her own share of troubles at the moment, and I just seem to be making things worse."

I looked around the diner to see which friend she was talking about, but the only person I saw who looked upset was Gabby Williams.

"Gabby? What's wrong with her?"

"I don't know. I figure you're one of her best friends, so maybe you'd know."

"What makes you say that?" I asked Trish softly. "I've known Gabby for years, but that doesn't make us friends."

"Come on, Suzanne. You're about the only person in town she even likes a little, and I see you two chatting every now and then. She's come to you before when she's been in trouble, so I thought maybe she said something this time."

"No, not a word," I said.

"Well, what are you doing just standing there? Go talk to her," Trish instructed.

Grace nudged me. "Yeah, go on, Suzanne."

"Aren't you coming with me?"

"You're kidding, right? The entire town knows how Gabby feels about me. No, I'm afraid that you're on your own this time. I'll just hang out up here with Trish while you talk to her."

"Fine," I said with a frown, and then I walked over to Gabby's table to see what was wrong. I supposed that I didn't really have any choice.

I had to just bite the bullet and do it.

CHAPTER 13

"**G**ABBY, ARE YOU OKAY?" I asked as I approached her table cautiously.

"What? Suzanne, what are you doing here?" she asked me as she looked up at me. "Did someone call you?"

"No. Honestly, I just came in for a bite, but I couldn't help noticing that you look troubled," I said. "May I join you?"

"Sorry, but I just finished eating," she said as she stood. "I'm fine."

"We both know that's a lie," I said forcefully. Maybe it was true about us being friends. After all, I was one of the few folks in town brave enough to actually confront her about anything.

Gabby looked as though she wanted to comment, but instead, she threw a ten-dollar bill down on the table and started to walk out.

She wasn't going to get rid of me that easily. I followed her. Trish's instincts had been right on the money.

"She forgot to pay," the diner owner told me as I got to her and Grace after Gabby had already walked out.

"She threw a ten-dollar bill on the table before she left," I said as I headed for the door.

"She didn't even wait for her change? This is more serious than I thought," Trish said. She wasn't teasing, either. Gabby was notorious about being tight with her money, and if she was willing to abandon money just to avoid talking to me, something was definitely up.

"I'll be right back," I said as I ducked out and followed her over to her shop, across the street and beside mine.

"Gabby. Hang on a second," I said.

"Are you deaf, Suzanne? I told you that I was fine," she insisted, not slowing her pace any at all.

I was younger and in better shape, though. I caught up with her before she made it to her shop. However, if she got inside and locked the door behind her, it was a lost cause, and we both knew it.

Gabby was just putting her key in the lock when I put my hand on the front door, preventing her from opening it.

"That's a good way to lose a hand," she said icily.

"I don't care. Friends don't let themselves be bullied out of caring." The use of the word surprised her as much as it did me.

Gabby sighed deeply, and then she turned to look directly at me. "Suzanne, I appreciate the concern, I truly do, but there's nothing you can do to help me."

"That's not true. I can listen," I said, standing my ground.

"I got dumped, okay?" she asked as she looked at me, tears starting to form in her eyes.

"I'm so sorry," I said. "I know that has to hurt."

"Have you ever been rejected by anyone?" she asked me with a real bite in her voice.

"Let's see. I caught my first husband cheating on me with another woman. Does that count?" I hadn't had to go far for that one.

"Yes, of course it does," she said. "I don't know why I bother trying to find someone. It seems rather hopeless at my age."

"If you really want it, it can still happen. Look at my mother." Momma had given up on romance in her life too, and yet Phillip Martin had pursued her with diligence and resolve, and now she was as happy as she'd been since my father had died.

"That's the difference between the two of us. No one's pining around town for me," Gabby said.

"You don't really know that though, do you? For all you know, someone may just be working up the courage to ask you out even as we speak."

Gabby frowned at me. "Are you saying that it would take an act of bravery to ask me out on a date?"

I could play that two ways, but there was a good chance either option would get me in hot water, so I decided to dive on in and tell the truth. "Gabby, you must realize that most folks around here are afraid to ask you what time it is. You have to know how intimidating you are."

To my surprise, she laughed at my assessment. "I've spent so long cultivating it for business that it's a part of me now, and I'm afraid that I'm too old to change."

"I don't believe that for one second," I said, happy that she'd taken my critique in the manner that it had been meant. "I personally know how nice you can be when you let your guard down."

"I don't know," she said, biting her lower lip after she said it.

"Look at it this way. What do you have to lose?"

"So let me get this straight," Gabby said. "I'm supposed to all of a sudden start being *nice* to people for no reason at all?"

"Hey, it's worth a shot, isn't it?"

"Let me think about it," Gabby said as she glanced over at the closed bookstore. "You found another one, didn't you?"

"Yes, somehow I seem to end up in the middle of murder much more often than I'd like."

"Do me a favor, Suzanne, could you?"

"Anything. Just name it."

"If you see my door standing wide open, send the police in first. I'd hate for you to be the one to find my body."

She wasn't joking as she said it, and I wondered if she'd been threatened lately. "Is something going on that I need to know about?"

"No one's said or done anything to me," she explained. "I'd just hate for you to see me like that."

In a way, it was a very sweet thing for her to say. "You've got a deal."

"And I promise that I'll do the same for you," she said.

How had this conversation suddenly turned so morbid? "Grace is waiting for me so we can eat. I'd better go, if you're sure you're okay."

To my surprise, Gabby reached out a hand and touched my shoulder lightly. For her, it was quite a display of affection. "Thanks for caring enough about me to say something."

"Hey, Trish was worried about you, too," I said.

"Not Grace though, right?"

There was no way I was going to walk into that trap. "I'll see you later. Remember, if there's anything I can do to help, let me know."

"Maybe I will," she said as she walked into ReNEWed and flipped the sign to show that she was now open for business yet again. It may have been my imagination, but I could swear that I saw her smiling through the front window when she thought no one was looking. Maybe Gabby would take my advice after all and let herself smile every now and then. I didn't believe that she had to have someone in her life to make her happy, but if *she* did, then I'd do everything in my power to help her make it happen.

"Suzanne, what a delight finding you here," Momma said after she and Phillip walked into the Boxcar Grill. Grace and I had only just been seated, so I was glad that I'd delayed our meal in order to speak with Gabby. "Grace, you're looking lovely as ever," Momma said. "May we join you?"

"That sounds great to me," I said. I didn't get to spend

nearly enough time with my mother, and Phillip had actually been growing on me lately. "Pull up a pair of chairs."

Phillip held a seat for Momma, and she accepted the act graciously. I had no idea why some women didn't like the courtesy. Jake did it for me when we went out to eat, and frankly, it made me feel special that he cared enough to make sure I was taken care of. Not that I didn't take care of him, too. That was one of the things I loved about our marriage. We were a true team, each striving to make the other one happy. I missed my husband, but I was going to try not to show it. Having this group sharing a meal was a happy thing indeed, and I planned on enjoying myself.

"I didn't realize that you two ever ate out," Grace said with a smile. "And why would you? Dot, you're one of the best cooks I know."

"Agreed," Phillip added quickly, and I was certainly in no place to deny it.

I loved Momma's cooking, but I got it. "It can get a little stale making meals every night," I said. "Everybody needs a break now and then."

"I offered to make chili, but she declined," Phillip said with a shrug.

"What is it with men and chili? It's the only thing they seem to be able to cook indoors," Momma said with a smile.

"That's not true. I make decent eggs, and my pancakes are good, too."

"True. I sit corrected," Momma said. "They make breakfast, too. Tonight, I'm going to splurge and forget about calories altogether."

"You look perfect to me just the way you are," Phillip said as he squeezed my mother's hand.

"Thank you, but we're both putting on a little weight, dear. We need to be a little more careful about what we eat." She paused for a long moment before adding, with a wicked smile, "But let's start tomorrow, shall we?"

The chief had been overweight when he'd started wooing my mother, but he'd done an excellent job paring down to his high school weight. However, domestic tranquility was clearly catching up with him, and it wouldn't surprise me at all to see the two of them walking around town for exercise as the weather started to warm up.

"If that's the case, then I'm going to make it count tonight," he said with a grin.

I had to laugh. It was good seeing this lighter side of him, something that had been sorely missing when he'd been the chief of police. Come to think of it, Jake had been a bit dour when he'd had the job temporarily as well, and Stephen was aging by the minute. It must have taken a real toll on them, and I was suddenly glad that I was a donut maker. Solving murder was just a hobby for me, and one that was beginning to grow stale for me.

"How about you, Grace?" I asked her. "Do you feel like indulging?"

"I'm willing to if you are," she said.

My jeans had been getting progressively tighter as winter had worn on, but I wasn't about to be the wet blanket of this particular party. "Then let's do this."

"Excellent," Phillip said. "Shall we start with a plate of fries for the table while we decide what we're going to eat?"

"On one condition," Momma said sternly.

Had she already changed her mind? "What's that?" he asked her.

"We have to get onion rings, too," she said with a happy smile.

At the rate we were starting out, I'd be lucky to make it home after dinner, and I only had a quarter-mile commute.

But I didn't mind one bit.

As the four of us worked our way through burgers, sides, and even a few milkshakes, we had a wonderful conversation between bites and sips.

Only near the end of the meal did Momma look directly at me and ask, "How's the investigation, Suzanne?"

I put off answering her by shoving the last onion ring in my mouth, but that would only delay my reply for so long. One thing was certain: it was insane to try to deny it. Not only had she probably already heard what Grace and I were up to, but even if by some miracle she hadn't, she'd still know the moment the first lie left my lips. "It's going slowly, but that's to be expected."

Momma grinned. "Well, look who's starting to grow up."

"Mother dear, I'm on my second husband and I own my own business," I told her. "I just assumed I'd already made it."

"All those things contribute, but when you stop lying to your mother, you're taking the final step into adulthood."

"When did *you* stop lying to your mother?" I asked her with a wicked grin.

"I suppose it became a moot point when she passed away," Momma said, adding a small sigh to highlight her regret.

"If you need any help with the case, you know we're both ready to be asked," Phillip said gravely.

"I thought you were only interested in *old* crimes," I said with a grin.

"I'll make an exception for you," he replied, his eyes smiling merrily at me.

"Thanks, but we're good. Right now, Grace and I have just finished interviewing our suspects."

"Ooh, who do you have so far?" Momma asked.

I ticked the writers off on my fingers and then added Abner to my list in the end, as well as Paige.

"Are you telling me that my mechanic wants to be a writer,

too?" Momma asked. "Is there *anyone* who doesn't aspire to write at least one book?"

"Funny you should mention that. As a matter of fact, your daughter turned the chance down last night," Grace said.

"Not that it matters one way or the other at this point," I said, and then I added, "John Rumsfield, aka the murder victim, wanted me to write a culinary mystery series for him."

"You should have taken him up on his offer," Momma said. "I've often thought it would be fun writing a cozy mystery. What do you think, Suzanne? We could write about a mother/daughter team of sleuths solving crime and making goodies, too."

"We both know that we'd kill each other before we managed to write the dedication," I said with a smile.

Momma laughed. "You are probably right. Who looks the most suspicious to you so far?"

"It's honestly too early to say," I told her. "Brad Winslow has a temper nearly as big as his ego. Bev Worthington and Simon Gant were about to be dumped by their publisher, and they weren't exactly thrilled about the prospect, no matter how much they both protested otherwise. Paige said that she heard that Alexa Masters was trying to get out of her contract, and Abner had a confrontation with the man hours before John was murdered. Here's the rub. The writers were all signed on with the man himself, not the company. With Rumsfield dead, it's not clear what happens now, though Brad claims that they're all free from any and all further obligations to the publishing house."

"My, my. What a mess. I still can't get over Abner."

"I know," I said. "Grace and I are having a hard time wrapping our heads around him as a killer too, but he thinks of his manuscript as his baby, and nobody is going to get away with showing it disrespect. According to Alexa, who watched the argument, John laughed in Abner's face, and then he flung the manuscript at him. Can you imagine that going over very well?"

"I doubt seriously that Abner murdered John Rumsfield," Phillip said quietly.

"Why? Don't you think he's capable of doing it?" Momma asked him, clearly curious about her husband's opinion.

"Oh, he's capable enough. I would think he'd be more of a strangler or a brawler, though. It would almost have to be something up close and personal. Besides, if he was going to kill the publisher, he would have done it at the height of his humiliation, not stew about it and then decide to do it later." He looked at me and saw that I was grinning. "Did I say something amusing, Suzanne?"

"Not at all. It's just that's pretty much the same conclusion Grace and I came to earlier."

"Not the strangling bit though, even though I like that twist," Grace added.

"What an odd lot we are," Momma said. She touched my hand lightly. "I'm so sorry you found another body, child."

"It doesn't get any easier," I said.

"Nor should it," Phillip answered. "With Jake being gone, if you need to talk about it, I'm here for you."

"I appreciate that," I said, and what was more, I meant it. "I'll be okay."

"When will your husband be back?" Momma asked me.

"When he and Terry are finished with their business," I answered.

"And that business is?" Momma asked, her last word hanging in the air an incredibly long time.

"All I was told was that it was personal. Terry saved Jake's life once upon a time, and he takes the debt seriously."

"As he should," Phillip said.

"And on that note, I believe it's time to make our way home, my dear. I couldn't eat another bite under gunpoint," she told her husband.

"I know," he said. "Isn't it great?"

I signaled for Trish so we could get the check.

Instead, the diner owner joined us and said, "It's already been taken care of."

"Trish, I can't let you keep buying me food, as sweet of you as it may be."

"I'm not," she answered with a grin.

"Momma," I said, ready to gear up.

"Actually, it's my treat," Phillip said, surprising me once again. "This was fun, ladies. Be careful, and remember, if you need us, we're just a phone call away."

My mother and her husband left the restaurant, with our thanks, and Trish walked us out as well. "They make a cute couple, don't they?" she asked.

"Yes, but the real question is, a couple of what?" I asked.

It was a joke, but it fell flat and no one reacted. Oh well. I couldn't be hilarious all of the time, I supposed.

We were heading to my Jeep when Grace tugged on my arm. "Suzanne. Look over there."

I checked to see where she was pointing, and then I saw Chief Grant nodding at Paige before he got into his squad car and drove off.

"Let's go see what's going on, shall we?" I asked her.

"Lead the way," she replied. "I'm right behind you."

CHAPTER 14

"**I** FINALLY GOT THE STORE BACK, though I'm not sure what good it's going to do me at this point," Paige said as we approached.

"You can open back up tomorrow morning and start fresh," I told her.

"Maybe. I don't know. I'm not sure. I know you said I'll get folks who want to see where someone was murdered, but I'm not positive I have the heart for it anymore."

"You could always try burning some sage to cleanse the place," Grace suggested.

Her suggestion surprised me. "Really? Do you believe in that?"

"I'm not sure myself, but I know a lot of people swear by it. One of my sales reps won't move into a new place without walking around with some burning sage. It's supposed to remove the bad juju or something like that. My attitude is, what can it hurt?"

"It's an intriguing idea, but I wouldn't even know where to begin," Paige said. "I'm willing to do it, but how do we go about it?"

"Let me call Ramona and ask her," Grace said. She dialed the number, and after a few minutes of hushed conversation, she hung up. "Okay. I've got it. First we need some sage."

"That much makes sense," Paige said. "Where are you

supposed to find it? Is it the kind you get at the grocery store, or is it some other type?"

"No worries on that count. She's bringing some with her when she comes," Grace said. "She couldn't wait to participate."

"How long will it take for her to get here?" I asked Grace, not sure how I felt about the ritual or how long I wanted to wait around to see what it entailed.

"Twenty minutes tops," Grace said.

I saw an opportunity to take advantage of our waiting time. "While we're waiting, would you mind if we had a look around inside the bookstore, Paige?"

"Be my guest. It's unlocked. If you don't mind, I'll wait out here for your friend."

"You honestly don't want to come inside your own bookstore?" I asked her. This really was serious, not that I could blame her. The murder had been so closely tied to her new bookstore that she couldn't separate the two in her mind. Maybe Grace was right about suggesting the ritual. I highly doubted how much actual cleansing the sage ceremony would do, but if it allowed Paige to distance herself from the murder, then it was something worth doing, no matter how skeptical I might be of the procedure. Besides, I could be wrong. Who knew? It might work miracles. If it did, I might have use of Ramona myself in the future.

Grace and I walked into the bookstore alone, and even after we flipped on all of the lights, it still felt dark and oppressive inside. It was almost as though Rumsfield's spirit was lingering behind, and he wasn't all that happy about being murdered the night before. If that were true, I really couldn't blame him.

"Did you feel that just now?" Grace asked me as we closed the door behind us.

"Feel what?"

"A cold, icy draft," she said with a shiver.

"You really believe in this stuff, don't you?" I asked her. As well as I knew Grace, it always amazed me that there were still layers I hadn't uncovered yet.

"I feel as though there is more to this world than we could possibly understand," Grace said. "There's a bad vibe in here, isn't there?"

"Maybe," I acknowledged. "If you want to wait outside with Paige while I look around by myself, I'm perfectly okay with that."

"No," she said after a moment's hesitation. "I'll stay here with you."

"Okay then," I said as I walked straight back to the break room where the publisher had been murdered. As I stepped between two sets of shelves, I felt a slight breeze of icy air myself, even though the windows were all closed and the bookstore was warm everywhere else. I decided to keep that particular experience to myself.

There wasn't anything as dramatic as a chalk outline on the floor where I'd found the body the day before, but it was almost as though I could still see it there on the floor without even closing my eyes and imagining it. The geode bookend was gone too, of course, and so was the bloodstained book I'd found by John Rumsfield's hand. Trying to drive the image out of my mind, I started looking at the other books close to where the body had been found.

They were all recent science fiction novels.

So how did the mushroom book make it there close enough for the publisher to reach before he perished?

I left the room and headed for the other storage area.

"You're not leaving, are you?" Grace asked as she closely followed.

"No, I want to check something out over here."

She was right on my heels, and I paused a moment to look at her. "What's up?"

"I thought I'd keep you company. You know, in case you get spooked or something," she said with a nervous laugh.

"Thanks. I appreciate that," I replied. I started searching the piles of books still scattered around the storage room, and it didn't take me long to find two other copies of *Seven Deadly Mushrooms*. The question was, how did the one I'd found near John Rumsfield get separated from the others? Why on earth had Paige ordered three copies of the field guide in the first place? It explained the overabundance of books everywhere. Evidently she hadn't been able to contain herself when she'd placed her initial order. I picked up one of the books and thumbed through it.

"What are you looking for?"

"Something, anything, that might explain why John Rumsfield would touch a copy of this book as he lay there dying," I said.

"I think Paige is right. He was pointing a finger from the grave at Brad Winslow."

"How many dying clues have we seen in real life?" I asked her.

"I admit that it's rare, but it still happens."

"And this book just happened to be close by? It couldn't have been more obvious unless the publisher had actually grabbed one of Brad Winslow's books on the shelf instead."

"Do you think someone is trying to frame him for murder?" Grace asked me softly.

"I'm beginning to think that it's a greater possibility than I did before seeing this. Remember, Brad told us that mystery writers tended to weave intricate plots when they write."

"That works against him, too, though, doesn't it?"

"What do you mean?" I asked her.

"What if he knew the police would suspect him, so he decided to frame himself in such a way that it lacked real credibility? It would be a clever way to take the attention off of him and shine it onto the other suspects."

I put the book back down in the pile as I tried to digest this new theory. "So you're saying Winslow killed his publisher, and then he grabbed a book from the other room that had a title similar to the ones he used, wiped the man's blood from his forehead onto the book, and then he staged it to look as though it were a dying clue?"

"It sounds absolutely insane when you put it like that," Grace admitted.

"But that still doesn't necessarily mean that it's wrong," I said.

"Are you saying that you actually believe it?"

"No, I'm not willing to go that far, but it's got to be a possibility," I replied. I looked around the storage room and spotted a stack of small, unopened boxes.

"What are those?" Grace asked me.

"Hang on," I said, and then I found what I was looking for. Conveniently, it was right on top of its own stack. I opened the lid and pulled out a geode bookend, one that looked remarkably like the murder weapon. "Whoever was back here must have spotted the mushroom book when they came to get the bookend."

"So then, it was planned after all," Grace said.

"Not extensively, if you ask me. Both significant things found near the body were taken from this room within a foot of one another. That means that the killer most likely was playing it all by ear as they went. It doesn't strike me as a properly planned-out crime at all. Does it you?"

"No, not unless someone's trying to be clever again," Grace admitted.

"You're right. It's harder than I thought it would be to figure out someone's methods whose mind automatically turns to intricate plots and clever devices. How are we ever supposed to find out who really killed the publisher if we keep spinning out these intricate scenarios?"

"We approach it just like we do every other murder we've ever investigated," Grace said. "We collect as many clues as we can, interview our suspects, and then we do our best to eliminate them one by one until we have the culprit in our sights."

"Is that all? You make it sound so easy, Grace."

"We both know that's not true in any way, shape, or form."

I was about to answer when I heard Paige calling us from outside the building. Evidently Ramona had made it to April Springs in record time.

"Thanks for coming out on such short notice," Grace told the young woman as she got out of her BMW. I'd been expecting a matron in a muumuu wearing enough crystals to weigh her neck down, but instead, this was a lovely, stylish young redhead with an expensive haircut and a quick smile.

"It's my pleasure."

Grace introduced Paige, and then she turned to me. "Ramona, this is Suzanne Hart."

The saleswoman took my hand and gave it a warm shake. "It's so nice to meet you. Grace has told me all about you. I'd love to try one of your donuts, but I'm afraid it would lead to a downward spiral of me binge eating them and not being able to fit into my clothes anymore."

"You should come by when I'm open if you like them that much," I said. "The first one's free." I suddenly remembered the donuts still in the Jeep. I'd never even gotten the chance to use them as bribes earlier, and I'd just have to throw them out tomorrow anyway. I was not a fan of stale donuts, and I'd rather see them thrown away than being consumed by anyone. "As a matter of fact, I can give you three dozen tonight if you'll walk over to my Jeep with me when we're finished here."

"As much as I appreciate the offer, I'd really better not," she said. After she collected some things from her trunk, she asked, "Shall we get started?"

"By all means," Paige said.

Ramona paused in front of her before heading to the bookstore. "I'm not making any promises, but I think you'll be amazed by how much good this does. By the time we're finished, I have a feeling that you'll see a real change in the atmosphere of this place."

"I hope so," Paige said, though her voice faltered a little at the end. She really was shaken up.

"It's going to be fine," Ramona said with such confidence that I began to wonder if there was something to this after all. I still wasn't sure how I felt about this ritual, but I immediately liked the woman performing it.

"What did you bring with you?" I asked her, curious despite my skepticism.

"This is the smudge stick," she said as she waved it around in the air. "It's made up of white sage and lavender."

"And the bowls?" Grace asked. "What purpose do they serve?"

"I use this one to hold under the stick as we walk through the bookstore. I probably don't need it, but we're going to be introducing fire into a place full of paper, so it doesn't hurt to be careful." Ramona handed the other bowl to me. "If you could fill this halfway with water, we'll use it to extinguish the sage if we need to. Some folks believe that you should let it burn out on its own, but I haven't found that to be the case at all."

"What can I do?" Grace asked, getting into the spirit of things.

"Go in ahead of us and open every window and door," she instructed. "That's also a point of contention among folks who smudge, but I believe it allows the negative ions to escape."

Once we'd done as we were told, we all met back at the front door, standing on the outside looking in. Ramona took out a lighter and lit the sage, letting it burn for a few seconds before blowing it out. The aroma was nice, an earthy-toned smell that reminded me of burning leaves, and the stick looked like incense as it smoldered, which I suppose technically it was.

She waved the smoking stick around the doorframe and intoned, "I cleanse this building of all negativity, all spirits of discord, all things in the spirit world that don't belong in this place of life, love, and laughter." After a few moments, she walked in, with the three of us right behind her. A part of me wanted to joke about the invocation, but the wiser part shut it down. I was surprised to see how seriously Paige was taking it, and Grace as well, for that matter.

There was a time to joke and tease, but this was clearly not it. Ramona walked around each room waving the sage stick as smoke from it drifted into the corners, around the windows, and even along the ceiling. As she moved, Ramona kept chanting, and she looked as though she might be in some kind of trance. The smoke dissipated, some of it floating out the windows. She spent the most time in the break room where the murder had occurred. Had anyone told her what had happened or where it had taken place? It was an odd thing. The smoke everywhere else had been thin and narrow, but in the room where the murder had occurred, it was visibly thicker and more tumultuous. Grace hadn't tipped her off, at least not while they'd been on the phone, and Paige hadn't had enough time before we'd joined them.

Finally, Ramona nodded, and then she called for the bowl of water, which I provided. Was it my imagination, or had the place gotten suddenly lighter? I couldn't honestly say, but I did feel as though a change had taken place. "Why did you focus on the break room the most?" I asked her before anybody else could prompt her as we walked back out front.

"I'm not sure. The mojo in there felt really strong, and the smoke was really rolling. I've never seen it do anything like that before, but I've read about it happening. Did something bad happen in there?"

"You didn't know? Why do you think Grace called you?" I asked her.

Ramona looked confused. "I do these cleansings for lots of people when they find a new place to live or move into a new business location. I just assumed she wanted me to clean the space for her friend. You didn't answer my question. Did something happen in that back room?"

"Someone was murdered there last night," Paige said haltingly. "I can't even get my clerk to come back in for work."

"That explains the tainted atmosphere inside," Ramona said. "The vibes are much better now though, don't you think?"

"It's truly amazing," Paige said. "I can't tell you how much better the space feels now. I must pay you for your time and trouble."

"Nonsense. I don't do it for money," she said.

"Then at the very least, pick out a book, with my gratitude."

"I did happen to spot a signed Alexa Masters. May I have one of those?"

"It would be an honor," Paige said. "Hang on. I'll go get it for you."

After she disappeared inside, Grace told her employee, "That was really something."

"I know; it is, isn't it? I've done the ritual two dozen times, but I've never seen a room in need of it so much as that back room. I'm glad I could help."

"Tell you what. I want to thank you, too," Grace said. "This was above and beyond the call of duty. Why don't you take tomorrow off? You earned it tonight."

"Are you sure? That would be great," she said.

"My donut offer is still good, too," I added, trying to add some lightness to the conversation.

"What can I say? I give up," she said with a laugh.

I was surprised that she'd taken me up on my offer after her earlier protests, but I was delighted that at least some of my spare treats would go to a good home.

"I'll meet you over there," I said.

I walked over to my Jeep, and Ramona was soon there in her car. She stopped and opened her trunk. "I've got three dozen I'm just going to toss tomorrow. Could you find good homes for them?"

"As a matter of fact, I volunteer at a seniors' facility in Lenoir, and I know that they'd love these."

"Then take them, with my compliments."

After I transferred them to her trunk, I asked her in private, "Ramona, just between us, what really happened in there?"

"I wish I could tell you, but I really can't quantify it," she said in all seriousness. "Suzanne, I get that you're skeptical about the process. I was too, the first time I saw it performed, but I have to tell you, it's amazing the difference the ritual makes. The bad energy seems to flow out, and it's replaced by new, fresh energy. Some people believe the sage produces positive ions that attract and cancel out the negative ones. I'm not entirely sure why it works, but I'm a firm believer that it does. I know I must sound insane to you, but the proof is in the results."

"After what I witnessed tonight firsthand, I'm willing to keep an open mind," I said.

"That's all anyone can ask," she said. "I already said good-bye to Grace and Paige. Have a good evening, Suzanne. It was a real pleasure meeting you."

"You, too," I replied, and then Ramona drove away, leaving me with more food for thought than I'd expected to have when Grace had first mentioned the sage smudging.

CHAPTER 15

"Wow, I feel like I just took part in an exorcism," Grace said as she sat in the passenger side of the Jeep in her driveway. I could have easily been home by now, but what rush was there? I'd eaten a good meal, done a little crime scene investigation, seen a smudging ceremony up close, and I still had time before my odd job sent me off to bed earlier than most folks ever dreamed about going to sleep.

"You looked pretty intense when it was happening," I said.

"I won't deny it. It was a little spooky seeing the way that smoke changed from room to room, but you know what? I honestly believe that I could feel a cloud lifting from the bookstore after Ramona finished. I always thought she was a little odd, but she showed herself in quite a different light this evening, didn't she?"

"Honestly, I'm not at all sure I'm ready to talk about what happened just yet," I admitted. "I still need some time to process it."

"I completely understand. Well, if you'd prefer, we could always talk about other things, like murder."

"It seems to be a frequent topic of conversation for us, doesn't it?"

"It does manage to come up with unusual regularity," she agreed.

"Much more than I like, as a matter of fact," I said.

"Tell you what. Why don't we forget about homicide for one night? Let's have one of our old-fashioned sleepovers. We can eat junk food and watch terrible movies until it's time to go to sleep."

"It's tempting, but I have to be up in seven hours," I said. "I'm not sure how much fun I would be, anyway. I'm exhausted. Could I take a rain check for a night when I don't have to get up in the middle of the night to go to work the next morning?"

"Absolutely. We'll have to pick a time that the guys are busy as well, though," Grace said. "I suppose anything's possible."

Evidently I'd hurt her feelings by refusing her gracious invitation. "You know what? I'm feeling better even as we speak. Tell you what. Let me call Emma and see if she and her mom can sub for me tomorrow. I know it's short notice, but they're always clamoring for more hours at the donut shop."

Grace stopped me before I could retrieve my phone. "Thanks for the offer, but we've got too much on our minds with the publisher's murder anyway, and like you said, you're worn out, with good reason. No worries. We'll make it happen another time."

"I'll make sure of it," I said. "What are your plans tonight? You could always watch a cheesy movie and eat junk food without me."

"I could, but what fun would that be?" she asked me with a grin. "If I'm taking the road to ruin, I'd just as soon not travel it alone." Grace sighed heavily, and then she added, "Besides, I've got a load of paperwork I need to at least take a stab at before bed. When did we get so old, Suzanne?"

"The way I look at it, it beats the alternative," I replied with a smile.

"I suppose it does at that," Grace said as she got out of my Jeep.

I drove the short distance up the road to the cottage I usually shared with my husband. I hadn't spoken to Jake in what felt like ages. What was my dear sweet husband up to, anyway?

After walking inside and locking the door behind me, I decided to give him a call. What was the worst that could happen? If it went to voicemail, at least he'd know that I loved him, and that I was thinking of him.

To my delight, he picked up on the second ring.

"You're not going to believe this, but I was just getting ready to call you," he said, and my mood suddenly lifted more than any sage smudge ever could manage to do.

"How's Raleigh? Have you had a chance to pop in on your sister and her kids while you've been there?" I asked him.

"No, it hasn't been that kind of trip. We've all been kind of tied up."

"That 'we' sounded like it involves more than two people. Can you still not tell me what you've been doing?" I asked him.

"As a matter of fact, that was why I was calling. Terry gave me the all clear, at least as far as you're concerned. He requested that you keep the information confidential."

"You know that I will."

"That's what I told him," Jake said with a laugh. "Terry's ex-wife has recently been mixed up with a pretty bad man, and he's worried about her. She fell off the radar last week, and there's been no sign of her since. He's pretty torn up about it, because he's been wanting to reconcile with her, but then this happened. He's desperate, Suzanne."

"He must be, if he asked you for help," I said. "Is this guy dangerous?"

"Very," Jake said. "And you were right about the 'we.' I'm not the only one lending a hand. There are four of us, actually.

We were all on the job together at one time or another, and two of us are still on active duty."

"Jake, this sounds really serious." I couldn't imagine how wicked this guy must be to require four state police inspectors to handle him. He must be another Jack the Ripper.

"Right now we're just trying to find her to see if she's being held against her will," Jake said, trying his best to reassure me and failing miserably at it. "If we find her and it comes down to some kind of confrontation, our presence is supposed to be more a show of force than anything else."

"Why don't I believe you?" I asked my husband.

"What can I say? We all owe Terry," was all he'd say in reply.

Ultimately, I knew that it had to be enough. "Just be careful, okay?"

"He told me to tell you not to worry. He said to say that he has my back."

"And you have his. I'm still going to worry though, and we both know it."

"That's what I told him you'd say."

"Seriously, how bad is the situation, on a scale of one to Attila the Hun?"

"I'd rate it about a seven," Jake admitted. "It's the way she disappeared that has us all stumped. We're working on some leads though, and I've got a hunch she's going to turn up pretty soon."

"Wow. Now I'm really worried." I took a deep breath, and then I asked him, "Do you think she's …okay?" I'd wanted to ask if he thought she was still alive, but I changed my mind at the last second. It was not the right question to ask.

"If she's not, I'm genuinely afraid of what Terry might do. This guy is going to need serious protection if anything happened to her. That's another reason we're all sticking close to him."

"You're a good friend and a good man, Jake Bishop," I told him.

"But not a very good husband," he said.

"What have you been doing to make you say something like that?" I asked him playfully. I was not worried about Jake's fidelity, though I'd never been able to say that about my first husband, Max.

"Well, for starters, I'm in Raleigh, and you're in April Springs."

"That's just a matter of logistics," I said. "You're with me in spirit, and that's what really counts. Speaking of spirits, I attended a séance of sorts tonight."

"A séance? You're kidding."

"Yes, of course I am. It was more like a cleansing of dead spirits using a sage smudging ritual."

After a long pause, Jake said, "I'd love to hear more about it. Whose spirit was it, anyway?"

That's when it occurred to me that my husband didn't know that I'd recently stumbled over another dead body.

"Do you have a few minutes? We've got some catching up to do," I said.

"For you, I'll make the time. Why don't you start at the beginning and go from there?"

After I finished bringing him up to speed, including the sage cleansing I'd witnessed, Jake let a deep sigh slip out. "I'll say this for you. You're never boring, are you, Suzanne?"

"I don't know what you're talking about. I'm just a simple donut maker at heart," I protested.

"Who happens to solve murders on the side," he added.

"Okay, I can't deny it. Grace and I have plenty of suspects and not much to go on. John Rumsfield was not a very popular man, and most of our suspects make their livings being clever and lying as a matter of course. Do you have any expert advice for me?"

Jake laughed before he spoke again. "Oh, no. I'm not about to fall into that trap. I'm sure you and Grace are doing fine on your own. Just remember, often the simplest answer is the right one, no matter how convoluted it might look at first."

"There's nothing simple about this case," I said. "Chances are good that whoever committed this crime spends their days thinking about ways to get away with murder. It certainly muddies the water."

"Focus on what you know, not what you might think," Jake said.

"Is that the sum total of your good advice?"

He laughed again. "Sorry, but that's all that I've got. You do my spirit good, Suzanne Hart Bishop."

"Right back at you," I said, fighting a yawn.

"Right now you need to get some rest. It will be time to make the donuts again before you know it."

"I know only too well how right you are. It was wonderful talking to you. Be careful now, you hear?"

"That advice goes double for you," Jake said. "Don't turn your back on any of them."

"Not a chance of that happening." Pausing for a moment, I added, "Let me know if you find her, okay?"

"You're worried about her, and you don't even know her. You're the one with the good heart, lady."

"Terry loves her, so there must be something good about her," I said. "Give him my love, will you?"

"Only if I get mine first."

"You've got it. Good night, Jake."

"Night, Suzanne."

Once we were off the phone, I started worrying that my husband was in a dangerous situation, but that had literally been his job description in his former career. Jake could handle himself, I knew that, and Terry was skilled as well. That still didn't stop me from worrying, but since it wasn't productive at the moment, I decided to try to put it out of my mind, along with trying to figure out who had killed John Rumsfield. I grabbed a quick shower, got into my jammies, and then I went to sleep.

Tomorrow would come soon enough, and I had a hunch that big things were about to happen.

I just wished that I had an inkling as to what they might be.

CHAPTER 16

"I'M SURPRISED TO FIND YOU here, Abner," I said as I unlocked the door to Donut Hearts the next morning so we could start serving our customers. The mechanic wasn't particularly fond of my treats, so I knew that his visit probably had more to do with our conversation the day before than his craving for treats.

"You need to leave me alone, Suzanne," he said angrily right out of the gate, clearly worked up about something.

"You're visiting me at my place of business. How exactly is it that I am the one bothering you?"

"Don't get cute with me. I'm talking about you and Grace coming by the shop yesterday and accusing me of killing that man."

I took a step back, and Emma came out. "Is everything okay out here?"

"So far, but it's too soon to tell if it will stay that way," I said.

"Should I call someone?" my assistant asked as she reached for her phone.

"There's no need of that," Abner said, the volume of his words lowering considerably. "We're just having a nice conversation."

"It didn't sound all that nice to me," Emma said, watching him carefully.

"It's fine," I said. "I'll call out if I need you."

"Okay, but I'm leaving the door open just in case," she replied before she headed back into the kitchen.

"You've got quite a loyal little lapdog there, don't you?"

"For your information, Emma is not only a great employee, but she's also one of my closest friends. Now you've said your piece, Abner, so unless you're shopping for donuts, it's time for you to go."

"I'm not nearly done," he said.

"Then get it over with, would you? We'll have customers coming in any second, and I don't want them to hear what you have to say."

"I didn't do it," he said firmly. "I'm sorry if I started yelling the second I walked in here, but it's really frustrating! I never touched that man, let alone smash him in the head with a rock!"

"And we're all supposed to take your word for it?" I asked him. Maybe it would be prudent to have Emma call the police after all. Then again, why not cut out the middleman? I had my own cell phone in my pocket. I started to reach for it when Abner started up again.

"You don't have to. I can prove it, Suzanne."

"I'm listening," I said, halting my motion.

"I heard the body was cold when you found it. Have they come up with a time for the murder yet?" he asked.

"Nobody's shared anything with me, but if I had to guess, I'd say it was sometime between nine and eleven p.m. You told me that you went home alone, drank some beer, and then went to bed. How could you possibly prove that?" The time of death was a rough guess based on when I'd found the body, the temperature it had been, and the last time anyone had seen John Rumsfield alive, so I was pretty certain I was at least in the ballpark. I'd have to ask the police chief later how close I was to being right.

"I didn't exactly tell you the truth before," he said. "I couldn't have done it."

"I'm still waiting for the proof," I said.

"I was at the Bentley the entire time," he admitted.

"What were you doing there?"

"Trying to break into Brad Winslow's room," he admitted.

"Why on earth would you do something like that?"

"When Rumsfield turned me down, I wanted a second opinion. If my book was no good, I needed to hear it from more than one person. You don't take a doctor's word that you're dying without getting someone else to weigh in, and Winslow's been in the business a long time."

"So you tried to break into his room to ask him for a critique?" I asked, curious about what his thought process must have been.

"Not at first. I kept pounding on his door, but he wouldn't answer. That's when I thought I might just make my way inside and wait for him to get back."

"How were you going to do that?" I asked, honestly curious at that point.

"Well, I couldn't just wait out in the hallway, could I? I read that you could take a credit card and slip it between a doorframe and the lock and jimmy a hotel room door open."

"Did it work?"

"No. I broke two cards trying," he said. "It's not as easy as they make it sound."

"What happened? Did you run out of credit cards?"

"No, somebody called the front desk on me, and before I knew it, some beefy guy had a hand on the back of my neck and was escorting me to a back room in the basement."

"Imagine that," I said. "They weren't happy about you trying to break into one of their rooms. Did they call the police?"

"Yeah, I spoke with them, too. All in all, I didn't get back home until after midnight."

"They just let you go?"

"What could they do? I broke my cards, but I never got in,

so they couldn't prove anything. That didn't keep them from trying to sweat a confession out of me, though. I kept my mouth shut, and they eventually decided to let me go."

"Without doing anything at all to you?"

He shrugged. "I'm not allowed back in the Bentley, but that's no big sacrifice. Anyway, I told you before, and I'm telling you again. I didn't kill that guy."

"So why did you lie to us yesterday?"

"I was embarrassed," he admitted.

"And you'd rather we think you might be a murderer than admit that you'd done something stupid?"

"I tried to break into a hotel room. I didn't kill anybody."

"You know what? I believe you," I said.

"You can call the police and check…Hang on. Did you just say that you believed me?"

"Why shouldn't I? It's not like your story can't be verified, and I understand not wanting to admit what really happened."

"Good. Then that's over with." He looked at the donuts behind me and added, "I feel a lot better now. Why don't you make me up a dozen donuts to go?"

"I didn't think you were a fan," I answered.

"They're okay, but the guys I work with really like them."

I wasn't going to stand there and try to talk him out of a sale, so I did as he asked.

Once he was gone, Emma came back out. "Wow. That was intense."

"You're telling me. Thanks for coming to my rescue."

"Of course. After all, it's what any good lapdog would do," she said with a frown.

"I don't know if you heard my response, but I told him

that you weren't just an employee; you were also a good friend of mine."

"I heard," she said with a slight smile. "Thanks for saying that."

"Why wouldn't I? After all, it's the truth. Today is going to be an odd one. I can feel it in my bones."

"I don't doubt it for one second. Hey, I just glanced at the calendar. Don't forget, you have a book club meeting today at ten."

"Thanks, I'd already forgotten all about it. Maybe I should cancel it."

"Are you kidding?" Emma asked me. "The ladies are going to love it. For once, they're involved in a real live murder."

"It's not nearly as glamorous as all that," I answered.

"That's because it's getting to be old hat for you."

"I hope that's never the case," I said.

Over the course of the next ninety minutes, I answered more questions than sold donuts, but I'd expected the trend to continue until a murderer was named. Folks wanted to feel as though they were in the know, and evidently I was the best source of information in town, though I was pretty reticent in my answers. Still, I managed to move some product, so the morning wasn't going to be a total waste.

Then, to my surprise, three people I never expected to see in my donut shop walked in together. Brad Winslow, Simon Grant, and Bev Worthington had all decided to pay me a visit at Donut Hearts.

CHAPTER 17

"**S**UZANNE, WE NEED TO TALK," Brad Winslow said, speaking for the group.

"If one of you is ready to confess to committing the murder, you might want to talk to the police instead of me," I said. That got the attention of a few of my customers, but when I looked in their direction, they quickly found other things to distract them, or so it seemed, though I knew that they were hanging on every word being spoken.

"We're not here to confess," he insisted. "We're going to solve the crime."

"I'm not sure that you can," I said, "and besides, why involve me?"

"We need you to get us into the bookstore," Simon said. "Paige won't let us in."

"Not with him with us, anyway," Bev said, looking at Brad.

"We had a huge blowout, okay?" the suspense writer said. "Paige is being petulant, but the three of us figured you might be able to talk some sense into her."

"We could always go in without you, Brad," Simon suggested.

"What good is that going to do you? *I'm* the one with the master plotting skills. If anyone's going to figure this out, it's going to be me."

"You don't have to be a decent outliner to write a good

mystery," Simon protested. "I *never* know who did it until I get to the end."

"And it shows in your prose," Winslow said. "I've heard your speech half a dozen times, remember? If you bring up that quote that if you don't know who did it, the reader never will, I'm going to throw up. At least your girlfriend here tries to outline her mysteries before she goes off half-cocked."

"I'm not his girlfriend," Bev said.

Brad looked surprised to hear the news. "Really? What happened?"

"We've decided to see other people, not that it's any of your business," Simon said.

"So, she dumped you," Brad said smugly.

"Watch it, hotshot," Simon replied. "There may be snow on the roof, but there's still a fire in the hearth."

Great. I was going to witness another brawl inside my donut shop. "Maybe you all should take your argument outside," I suggested.

"Not without you," Brad insisted. "Paige will listen to you. Ask her to let us in. It's to her advantage, and yours, too."

"Why should I care whether you get in or not?" I asked them, doing my best to feign innocence.

"You're trying to solve the crime too, dear, so there's no use trying to deny it," Bev said.

"We know why you came by the Bentley and started asking questions," Brad added. "We're not fools, Suzanne."

"It didn't take us long to find out that you've done this before," Simon supplied. "So, what do you say? Will you help us? It's probably a lost cause getting Paige to let all of us in, but we figured if anyone could do it, you could."

They were right. I was curious to get four of my main suspects back to the murder scene. I was keeping Paige on my list, since she had everything but motive, at least that I knew of.

I didn't know what it might be, but that didn't mean she didn't have one. That made me wonder where the final writer might be and why she wasn't with the group. "Why isn't Alexa with you?"

"She refused. She claimed that she wasn't interested in playing detective," Brad said derisively. "In my mind, that's suspicious behavior in and of itself."

"Or it could mean that she has reasons of her own not to want to revisit such an unpleasant place," Bev said.

"I agree with Bev," Simon chimed in.

"Stop sucking up to her, man. Have a little pride. She's not taking you back," Brad chided.

Simon's face reddened. "I really do agree with her."

"What do you say, Suzanne? Will you help us?" Bev asked.

"I'll try," I said. "Wait for me out front. I need a minute."

"You can have thirty seconds, and then we're going to try again without you," Brad said.

Once they were gone, I opened the kitchen door and found Emma hard at work cleaning up. "Would you mind watching the front for ten minutes or so?"

"I'd be happy to," she said. "What's up?"

"I'm going to try to get into the bookstore with three of the writers from last night."

"And they need you to get them in?"

"Something like that," I said.

"Fine, but don't forget your book club meeting."

"I should be back in plenty of time for that," I said. I took off my apron and joined the writers, who had, to my surprise, obeyed my request and waited for me, despite going over the promised minute after all.

As we crossed the street together, I said, "Let me do the talking, okay?"

"I'm the spokesman for the group," Brad protested.

"That's funny. I don't remember taking a vote," Bev said.

"Besides, you couldn't get us in the first time. What makes you think you'll have any luck now?" Simon asked. "Let Suzanne have a crack at it."

"Fine," Brad said sullenly.

I knocked on the door, but Paige wouldn't open it, though I could see her through the glass sidelights. "We're closed. Sorry. You'll have to come back later."

"Paige, it's Suzanne. Can we talk?"

"That depends."

"On what?"

"Are you alone?" she asked.

"You know I'm not. Give me a chance to talk, okay?"

I wasn't sure she was going to open the door, but finally, it split open a crack. "Why should I let them in, Suzanne? They've all been nothing but trouble since they came to town."

"I know you have a history with Brad, but don't forget, they all solve mysteries for a living. Wouldn't you like to know what really happened to John Rumsfield?" I asked her. "Maybe they can help."

"They *write* mysteries, they don't solve them," she corrected me. "I'd be okay with Bev and Simon, but Brad's not coming in."

He started to protest when Bev put an elbow into his ribs. Good for her!

"We need him, too. Please?" I asked.

Paige took a full thirty seconds to decide, but finally, the door opened the rest of the way. "You have ten minutes, and that's just because you and Grace brought Ramona here last night."

"Thanks," I said, and then I turned back to the writers. "Come on. Let's go. We don't have much time."

They walked into the bookstore single file, and I noticed that when Brad got close to Paige, she shot him a look that was full of death and daggers. The two really had gone through a falling out. At the signing, she'd found a way to even be pleasant to the man, but something had clearly changed since then. I didn't have time to figure out what it might be, though.

I had a crime scene to explore with three mystery writers.

I couldn't wait to see what they had to say and to see if maybe one of them would be a little too clever and give themselves away.

I wasn't at all surprised when they headed straight for the break room where I'd found John Rumsfield's body the day before. Had it really been that recent? A part of the experience felt like a distant memory, but being back there again brought it all to the forefront, despite the cleansing ceremony I'd participated in the night before.

"Now, the way I see it, there are one of three possibilities," Brad said, surveying the room.

"What are our options in your mind?" Simon asked him.

"The murder was either planned, it was committed on the spur of the moment, or it was made to look that way."

"It could have been a case of mistaken identity," Bev offered.

"Why do you say that?" Simon asked her.

"Brad and John had the same basic build. If it was dark in here, someone could have mistaken him for our publisher and conked him in the head by accident." She looked intently at Paige as she said it.

"He was struck from the front, remember?" Brad asked. "Are you this sloppy in your books?"

"Her novels happen to be great," Simon said.

No one seemed to care. After a moment, Brad asked, "Suzanne, where exactly did you find the body?"

I pointed to the floor where I'd found him.

"I'm having a difficult time visualizing it. Would you mind lying down in the exact spot?" Brad asked.

"No. Absolutely not. I'm not going to do that," I said firmly.

"Simon, you do it," Brad ordered.

"I'm not keen on doing it, either. Besides, I didn't see where he was lying any more than you did. Unless you were the one who killed him."

"That's garbage, and you know it. Let's try to picture it, then. Suzanne, could you describe it to us?"

I suddenly realized that I could do better than that. I'd taken a few photos with my phone when I'd found the body, but the stress and trauma of it all had made me forget momentarily that I'd even done it. At least I'd remembered to show Grace, and the police surely had their own set of photos, but I hadn't referred to them since I'd shown my partner in crime. Some investigator I was turning out to be.

"I can do better than that," I said as I pulled out my phone. After bringing up the three pictures I'd taken, I showed them to the group, one after another. They were of the man himself, the bloodied bookend, and the marked book, in that order. Brad grabbed my phone when I made my way back to the image of John Rumsfield. "How do you explode this image?"

"You do this," I said, grabbing it back and using my finger and thumb to increase the image size on the small screen. "What do you want to see?"

"I want to go back to that book," Simon said. "What's the title?"

"*Seven Deadly Mushrooms*," Paige said with some satisfaction from the doorway. "Quite the coincidence, wouldn't you say, Brad?"

"Why? I didn't write it!"

"Maybe not," Simon said, "but it does use the word *deadly*, doesn't it? That's a favorite of yours, isn't it, Brad?" It was clear he enjoyed zinging his fellow author.

"It was probably just the closest book to the body," he said. "That doesn't prove anything."

"But it wasn't," I said. "I found the other two copies on

hand, but they were both in the storage room across the hallway, along with the rest of the extra nonfiction."

"It still doesn't mean anything. It's just a coincidence," Brad protested.

Simon turned to Bev. "How many times have we heard him on this book tour say that there was no such thing as a coincidence?"

"In a book, you moron, not in real life," Brad shouted. "Hang on. Let me see the image of John again."

I held it up to him, but I didn't relinquish possession of my phone.

"Zoom in on his hands. Find the one with the blood on it," he ordered.

I would have refused, but I wanted to see where he was going with it myself.

"There. That proves someone was trying to frame me!" Brad crowed.

"Why do you say that?" Simon asked as he and Bev craned to see the image. I noticed that Paige herself was trying to get a glimpse of it, and she somehow managed to bury her distaste for her former beau long enough to get closer to the small screen.

"The blood is on his right hand," Brad said triumphantly.

"So?" Simon asked.

"He was left-handed, you simpleton, or didn't you ever notice?"

Simon shook his head. "I didn't, but that doesn't make me stupid."

"I didn't know that, either," Bev said, surprising them both by backing Simon up.

I suddenly remembered that the publisher had poked Brad in the chest with his left index finger, indicating his dominant hand, and not his right. The author was on the money, and somehow I'd missed it completely.

"Why does that even matter?" Paige asked.

"If he were lying there dying, would he reach out with his weak hand to leave a clue? I can't imagine, especially since it would have been easier for him to reach out with his left hand. Someone wanted to make it look as though I killed him."

"That's one theory," Paige said. "Then again, maybe you did it, and he did his best to leave a dying clue."

"I'm telling you, it's an attempt to frame me!" Brad insisted.

"Brad, you might not be the most pleasant man in the world, but who would want to frame you for murder?" I asked.

"I can think of one person," he said as he turned to glare at Paige.

The bookstore owner looked startled by the accusation. "That's ridiculous."

"Is it?" Brad asked. "After our fight, you could have done it just to get back at me for rejecting you again."

Her face brightened as she blushed. "That was just too much wine talking," she protested. "Besides, I saw him last when you did. We were at my place most of the night, or have you already forgotten about that?"

What? This was indeed news. "Exactly what time were you together?" I asked.

"I'm not exactly sure that's any of your business, Suzanne," Paige said.

"I'm not asking out of some sense of prurient interest," I said. "This is important. I'm trying to see if you two have alibis."

"We started talking a little before nine," Brad said.

"And he didn't leave my place until well after one a.m.," Paige replied. "He was ready to reconcile at ten, but by eleven, he said he'd changed his mind. We argued for two hours, and then he stormed out. That's what he's best at, you know."

"I don't need to know any more than that," I said, hoping they wouldn't choose to share any more details with us than they already had. "Whether you realize it or not, you both have alibis for the time of the murder."

"Unless they did it together," Simon said.

"Agatha Christie wrote something like that once," Bev added.

"We didn't kill him!" Paige said. "Can you imagine me doing *anything* with that fool? I'm just sorry that I'm the one who's going to clear his name."

"I care deeply for you as well, Paige," Brad said smugly.

Evidently that was the last straw. "Get out of my shop!"

"Come on. Lighten up," Brad said, trying to smooth things over with her.

"I said get out and I meant it. All of you!"

There was no questioning the sincerity of her command. We all left the bookstore, but before I could apologize for making her admit to what she'd done the night of the murder, Paige slammed the door in my face. Once this was all over, I had some serious fences to mend there, but I couldn't worry about that at the moment.

Brad looked at us all and grinned. "You heard the lady. I've got myself an alibi." He paused as he studied Bev and Simon for a moment before adding, "Unless my count is off, that just leaves the two of you."

"Don't forget Alexa," Bev said.

"Of course you're right. So, we have it narrowed down to one in three. I like the odds."

"*Anybody* could have killed John Rumsfield," Simon protested. "It doesn't necessarily mean that any of us did it. I'm quite sure he's been making enemies for years."

"But no one else is around," Brad said. "Not that it matters to me."

He took off walking down the street.

"Where are you going, Brad?" Bev called out.

"I'm going to have a nice little chat with the chief of police, and then I'm getting out of this town, and I'm never coming back."

After he was gone, Simon looked at Bev. "Should we go back to the hotel?"

"We might as well," she said. "I'm glad you drove us here."

"What about Brad?" I asked.

"Let him get his own ride back to the Bentley," Bev said. "Personally, I hope he has to walk the entire way."

After they were gone, I realized that Brad had probably been right. Our field of suspects had now been narrowed down to one of three writers.

Which one was a murderer in real life though, and not just on paper?

There was nothing more I could do at the moment, so I walked across the street to relieve Emma from her duties at Donut Hearts.

Sometimes it was nice having a semblance of sanity in a world that appeared to have gone completely mad.

CHAPTER 18

"WHERE HAVE YOU BEEN?" JENNIFER asked me as soon as I walked into Donut Hearts. Elizabeth and Hazel were already there as well.

I glanced at my watch. "Am I late? I didn't think we were meeting for another twenty minutes," I said.

"We couldn't wait, not after what happened after we left the bookstore last night," Elizabeth said.

"You must have been terrified," Hazel added. "I can't believe you found another body, Suzanne."

Why did everyone keep saying that? Was I becoming some kind of dark omen, finding bodies wherever I went? "Me, either," I said, waving to Emma and then taking my seat. The ladies already had their treats and coffee, and my lovely assistant brought me a mug as well.

"Want anything to go with that, boss?" she asked me with a smile.

"No, this is good." I took a deep sip, and then I turned to find my fellow club members still staring at me. "Don't worry, it's not contagious."

"We didn't think it was," Jennifer said. "Should we go ahead and get started?"

"Let me just duck in back and grab my books," I said. "I'm interested in discussing detailed plotters versus spontaneous writers today. It should be really interesting comparing and contrasting the two styles."

"Actually, there's no need to get them at all," Elizabeth said. "If it's all the same to you, we want to jettison the book discussion this month entirely."

"Why would we want to do that?"

Jennifer took a deep breath, and then she explained, "It seems a little silly talking about a few made-up murders when there was a real one right across the street less than thirty-six hours ago. If it's too painful for you to discuss though, we don't have to talk about it."

Jennifer may have said it, but it was clear that they all wanted to talk about what had happened to John Rumsfield. I might get away with brushing off other people, but these women were my friends. "Okay. It's fine by me. What do you want to know?"

"What made you go into the bookstore in the first place?" Hazel asked me.

At nearly the same time, Elizabeth asked, "Was there much blood?"

While Jennifer said, "I'd love to hear all of it."

"Okay," I said, lowering my voice so the folks nearby wouldn't be subjected to my retelling the experience. "I was driving to work when I saw that the front door of the bookstore was open across the street. I called the police, but while I was waiting to be connected, I could swear I heard someone inside."

"Was the killer still inside?" Jennifer asked, hanging on every word.

"No, it was most likely just my imagination. Evidently John Rumsfield had been dead for hours by the time I found him."

"So that explains why you went in by yourself. You wanted to investigate in case someone was in trouble," Hazel said approvingly.

"That's why. Anyway, I started flipping lights on as I worked my way to the back, but the one in the break room wouldn't come on, so I turned on my heavy-duty flashlight, and I used it to look around. I saw something on the floor that I didn't recognize. As a matter of fact, at first I thought it was a painter's tarp or something, but the closer I got, I started realizing that it was a dead body."

"I can't imagine how that must have felt," Elizabeth said. "We read about murder all of the time in our books, but I can't imagine actually seeing a dead person up close."

"At least I didn't witness the crime itself," I said. "I just saw the results."

"Still, I can't help but be curious about it," Jennifer said. "We all are."

"I took a few pictures with my cell phone, but I don't think you'll like them," I told the ladies. I knew that I shouldn't have mentioned the photos the moment the words left my lips, but it was too late to take them back now.

"They're on your phone? Still?" Hazel asked, clearly a little unsettled by the idea.

"It's instinct for me to record the crime scene at this point," I said. "I wanted to document what I found."

Elizabeth asked in a soft voice, "Can we see them?"

"I don't know. One of the shots is kind of disturbing," I warned them.

"We're grown women, Suzanne," Jennifer said. "We can take it."

"Hazel? What do you think?"

She looked down at her hands, started to reluctantly nod in agreement, and then she abruptly stood up. "I thought I could do it, but it turns out that I can't. I'll wait for you outside."

"We don't have to look, either," Elizabeth said, imploring her friend not to leave.

"It's probably not a good idea, anyway," Jennifer added.

Hazel was not to be dissuaded. "No, you both want to see them. That's fine with me, as long as I don't have to look. I'll wait out in the car for you."

I couldn't stop her, and in a moment, she was gone.

"I'm sorry I mentioned it, ladies," I told the other two. "I didn't mean to upset Hazel."

"She'll be okay," Jennifer said, and then, after taking a deep breath, she added, "I'm ready. How about you, Elizabeth?"

She nodded in agreement, and I knew that I couldn't back out of it now, no matter how much I wanted to tuck my phone back into my pocket and forget all about it. I chose to show them the bloodied book first, it being the least offensive of the lot.

"I have to say, that's more than a little disturbing in and of itself. Seeing it in the movies or reading about it is one thing, but that's someone's real-life blood there," Elizabeth said with a frown.

"Is it significant to the case?" Jennifer asked.

"That's still to be determined. Listen, you two. We don't have to go on."

"No, we can handle it," Elizabeth said, and Jennifer simply nodded.

I pulled up the bookend next.

"That's what the killer used?" Jennifer asked softly, her voice barely above a whisper.

"Yes, so it seems," I admitted. I saw that she'd turned a little green around the gills. "What's wrong?"

"I bought that same bookend for her at Christmas two years ago," Elizabeth said.

"I'm sorry, but after seeing that, I'm not at all certain that I'll ever be able to look at them again," Jennifer said apologetically.

"I know I wouldn't keep them if I were you. Throw them away, donate them, stick them in your attic for all I care, but for goodness sake, don't leave them out. I'll buy you something to replace them."

"That's sweet of you to offer, but no thanks," Jennifer said.

Both women looked shaken up, and I was about to refuse

to show them John Rumsfield's body when Elizabeth said, "Suzanne, if it's all the same to you, I believe that I'll skip the last one. I need some air."

"I'll go with you," Jennifer said.

Both women stood, and as they headed for the door, I began to apologize. "I'm so sorry. Please forgive me. I don't know what I was thinking."

"There's nothing to forgive," Jennifer said as she stopped. "We practically begged you to show us. We just weren't ready to see them after all."

"I don't know how you even function after seeing something like that in real life, up close and personal like that," Elizabeth added.

"I didn't ask for it; it was just bad luck on my part."

"But you're still digging into what happened, aren't you?" Jennifer asked me in all seriousness.

"I found the body. That makes me vested in figuring out who did it in my mind. If they get away with it, then the nightmares will be for naught."

"You're having nightmares?" Elizabeth asked, and then she corrected herself immediately. "Of course you are. Why wouldn't you?" She then turned to our leader and said, "I've suddenly lost my appetite for murder, fictitious or otherwise. I'm taking off."

"I'm right behind you," Jennifer agreed.

Was I losing them forever because of my thoughtless offer to show them crime scene photos? "You're coming back, aren't you?"

"Not today, but next month, certainly," Jennifer said, and then she patted my hand. "I'll email you about the next book selection in a few days. Better yet, maybe I'll stop by and we can have some coffee and a treat, just the two of us."

"I'd like that very much," I said.

After they were gone, I wondered about my own reaction to what I'd found earlier. Hazel, Elizabeth, and Jennifer were smart, strong, well-balanced women, and yet they hadn't even had the stomachs to view a photo of the murder victim's body. What did that make me, someone who could not only see it but remember to take photos of it in the moment, and the rest of the crime scene? Had I become so inured to what I'd done in the past that it didn't affect me as much anymore? If I'd grown that hardened, then maybe this should be the last murder I ever investigated, no matter what the circumstances might be. I yearned for the time of innocence I'd felt before I'd found my first body, that of a customer and friend, Patrick Blaine, dumped in front of my shop. Since then, I'd been on a spiraling decline where dead bodies were not nearly as rare as they once were. Maybe it was time to take a step back and reevaluate my life choices.

But I wasn't going to even consider it until after John Rumsfield's killer was unmasked.

CHAPTER 19

"I S IT CLOSING TIME YET?" Grace asked me as she came into Donut Hearts just before eleven.

"We still have ten more minutes, and seven donuts left to sell," I told her.

"If I buy all seven, will you lock the door now?" she asked me with a wicked grin.

"Done and done," I said with a smile. "As a matter of fact, you don't even have to buy the donuts."

"I don't mind a bit. Keep the change," she said as she slid a ten across the counter.

"Do you really want them?"

"Who knows? I might get hungry later tonight. Box them up."

I opened the kitchen door and called back to Emma, "Do you have any problem with us shutting down early?"

"Let me think about it. No," she said instantly afterward with a grin.

"That's what I figured," I replied.

I boxed Grace's donuts and set them aside, and then I started my shutdown procedure. As I ran the register report, I counted the money in the till, and we came out even to the penny. I hadn't rung Grace's ten up, and when Emma joined us, I handed the bill to her.

"What's this for?" she asked.

"Grace is buying you lunch today," I replied. "Isn't that sweet of her?"

"Thanks, Grace," Emma said, folding the bill up and stuffing it into her jeans without even asking us why.

"You're most welcome," she said.

I finished filling out my deposit slip, and as Emma headed for the door, she asked, "Do you want me to drop the deposit off on my way?"

"That would be great," I said as I handed her the bag.

Once she was gone, Grace asked, "So, what have you been up to this morning?"

"What makes you think I've been doing anything?"

"Suzanne, we've been friends too long for you to try that with me. You know something, and what's more, you've been dying to tell me since I first walked in the door. I'm a patient woman, but even I have my limits."

"Really? Do you honestly consider yourself patient by any definition of the word?" I asked her, smiling.

"Okay, not so much, but things have been happening. Am I right, or have I misread the situation?"

"No, you're correct. You'll never believe who came into the donut shop this morning."

She raised an eyebrow as she asked, "Maybe not, but are you really going to make me guess?"

"No. Abner came by first thing, and it turns out that he has an alibi."

"Don't tell me he was involved in some kind of secret liaison," Grace said.

"No, actually, he was in hotel jail. He tried to break into Brad Winslow's room, and he got caught. Before you ask why he was doing a little B&E on the side, it turns out he was going to brace the author to convince him to read his manuscript after John Rumsfield refused to give it more than a cursory look."

"That sounds like something Abner would do. How did Brad react to the intrusion?"

"He wasn't there," I said. "Evidently he and Paige were having one last fling, though Paige didn't think that was what it was at the time. They had a huge fight afterwards, and they were still arguing even while the publisher was being murdered."

"My, you have been a busy little bee," Grace said. "I'm surprised you had time to sell any donuts at all today."

"That's not even all of it. Brad, Simon, and Bev came by the shop, and we went over to see if the writers could figure out who killed John Rumsfield for themselves."

"And Paige just let you all into the bookstore, even Brad?"

"She was reluctant at first, but I didn't know why until she and Brad had another fight, this one in front of the rest of us."

"Man, I knew I should have called in sick today and hung out with you," she said. "Did the liar's club come up with anything?"

"It seems they agree that it was either a rash, unpremeditated act, a deliberate murder made to look like a frame job, or a case of mistaken identity."

"Wow, that covers a lot of ground. I'm stunned no one suggested Rumsfield tripped and fell, hitting his head on the bookend on his way down."

"That never came up," I said, "but it's probably as good a theory as any at this point. I wonder why no one thought of that."

"Probably because an accident doesn't make it murder, and those three probably always have homicide on their minds, since it's how they earn their livings. Where was Alexa when all this was going on?"

"Evidently she refused to participate. She thought they should let the police handle it, since it was a real-life murder and not a fictional one."

"I bet that didn't make her very popular with the rest of the group," Grace said. "It kind of makes her look a little guilty, doesn't it? I know there's a popular belief that murderers like to revisit the scene of the crime, but I can't imagine going back to a place where I killed someone."

"I can't, either," I said. "At least we've narrowed our field of suspects down to Simon, Bev, and Alexa now."

"Assuming it was one of the writers on the panel who did it," Grace said. "We both met John Rumsfield, and neither one of us was particularly taken with the man. I can't imagine he'd have such a narrow list of folks who might want to see him dead."

"Probably not, but as far as we know, they were the only ones in town, and evidently his trip was planned at the last minute, so no one else had any warning that he'd even be here."

"So, what do we do now? Do we brace the last three of our suspects again?"

I glanced out the window at the bookstore across the street, which was now open to the public again. "We probably should, but I'd like to have a little ammunition before we do. There's only one problem with that, though."

"Only one?" Grace asked me with a grin. "I'd say we were doing pretty well, if that's the case."

"Okay, more than one, but one that's immediate. I need some advice and information from Paige, but after what happened earlier, I'm not sure she'll be all that predisposed to giving it to me."

"There's only one way to find out then, isn't there?" Grace asked. "Put on your big-girl shorts and let's go ask her. Are you ready to eat a big crow sandwich?"

"I don't really have much choice," I said.

"Then let's do it."

I noticed that Grace hadn't taken her box of donuts with her. "Can I buy those back from you?"

"Getting hungry already?" she asked me.

"No. I just thought a peace offering might be in order."

Grace nodded in approval. "Take them, with my blessings. It's a great idea."

"Hey, donuts have gotten me into more doors than my winning personality ever has over the years."

"And why wouldn't they?" she asked, before quickly adding, "Not that you don't have your own set of charms as well."

"Thanks for adding that, even if it was barely just in time to take the sting out of your first comment."

"Glad to. After all, what are friends for?"

We walked across the street and into the shop. Paige's smile of greeting quickly evaporated when she saw that I was back.

Before she could throw me out again, I decided to make a preemptive strike. "Would you accept a peace offering from me for earlier?" I asked her as I held the partially filled box out to her. I would have preferred to have an even dozen, but beggars couldn't be choosers.

Paige frowned, and then a smile slowly crept to her face. "That depends. What have you got?"

"I admit that it's just a partial assortment," I said as I handed her the box.

She opened the lid and glanced inside. "Why do I have the feeling that these are all of the donuts you didn't sell today?"

"That's not true at all," I said with a smile. "I sold those, too. Grace bought them, but we decided they'd be put to better use giving them to you."

"Thanks, Grace," she said. "I appreciate it. Would you care to join me in one?"

"Why not?" Grace asked as she surveyed her choices.

I just stood there awkwardly until Paige glanced over at me. "I'd offer you one, but you're probably sick of them by now."

"Think again," I said as I grabbed one of the plain glazed donuts. We should have brought napkins, but I wasn't above licking my fingers after I finished.

Paige laughed at me, and the tension seemed to break between us.

"I really am sorry I was a part of that this morning," I said.

"I know you were just an innocent bystander," she said. "I shouldn't have taken it out on you."

"Want the chance to make it up to me?" I asked her.

"What did you have in mind? I can give you a free book, if you'd like."

"I'd rather have some insights," I said.

"Those I can supply easily, though I don't know what I can tell you that you don't already know. I only really know Brad, and it turns out that most of the things I thought I knew about him were wrong."

"My book club got me thinking about something earlier," I said. "We were supposed to discuss people who write based on careful outlining and those who create the story as they go."

"It's an age-old debate among writers, plotters versus pantsers," she said.

"Do you know much about the writing processes for Simon Gant, Bev Worthington, and Alexa Masters?" I'd picked up a few snippets here and there, but it would be nice to have outside confirmation from someone in the business.

"More than I ever need to," she admitted. "When I found out they were coming to The Last Page with Brad, I did a ton of research on them all."

"Then you're exactly the person we need to speak with," I said.

"What does this have to do with John Rumsfield's murder?"

"Maybe nothing. Maybe everything," I said. "Would you indulge me?"

"Sure. Alexa is a true outliner, from what I've read. She uses index cards for everything, and by the time she was ready to start writing her first book, she had seven shoeboxes full of them. Bev is another plotter. Supposedly she uses a plot wheel to come up with her victim, the killer, a list of suspects, and everything else she might need to know. She started as a cookbook writer Rumsfield recruited to write culinary mysteries for him, and it's clear if you read her books that she's far better with the recipes than she is with the stories she tells. They have a sameness to them that makes me feel as though she found one plot, and she keeps recycling it from book to book. I'd say that she's the least creative when it comes to her plot devices. They are extremely simple, and there aren't any twists and turns in her mysteries at all. Simon is the opposite end of the scale. He claims that he comes up with the barest seed of an idea first, and then he sits down to write without having any idea where he's going. He claims that he tried to outline once, but he couldn't write the book, since he already knew how it turned out, and that was the real reason he wrote, to amuse himself."

"Okay, that's all good information," I said, nodding as I realized that it all fit in to a theory that I'd been toying with since the night before. I had a sudden thought. "Paige, have you ever considered starting a book club here? Or even more than one? You could host one every Thursday night. Mystery could be one week, romance another, science fiction a third, and general literary stuff on the fourth. It would give the most avid of your readers an excuse to come back at least once a month, and while they were here, they'd be bound to pick up some of your latest offerings."

"That's brilliant," she said. "Do you mind if I steal your idea completely?"

"You can't steal something that's being freely given," I said. "Are we good?"

"We are," she said. "Thanks again for the donuts, ladies."

"You're most welcome," Grace and I said in unison.

"What was that all about?" Grace asked me once we were back

outside again. "I'm not sure if you suspect the plotters or the pantser. If you take the crime as one of impulse, then it's Simon you suspect, but if it's a carefully staged murder meant to look like a frame, then one of the plotters must have done it."

"I'm still undecided," I said, "but I think we can rule Bev Worthington out, at least for the moment. If she uses only one plot, I doubt she'd be creative enough to come up with a frame or to carry it through even if she could plan it. From everything we've learned, she's a cookbook writer at heart, not a mystery author. If she did this on the fly, she wouldn't have been calm enough to try to frame Brad Winslow, and I can't see her striking the publisher in the heat of the moment, either. If anything, she seemed relieved to leave her detective behind and try her hand at writing something different."

"So, for the moment let's assume that you're right. That leaves Alexa and Simon."

"We don't know enough about Alexa's style after only one book, but if she was planning to frame Brad Winslow with that deadly mushroom book, she failed to execute her plan properly. Whoever marked that book with John's bloody fingerprint used the wrong hand. Does that strike you as a detail a meticulous planner would miss?"

"Maybe she's better at murder on paper than in real life," Grace suggested.

"You've got a point. The women from my book club wanted to see the crime scene photos I took on my phone, but they never even made it all the way to the body."

"That reminds me. There's something I want to check in one of those shots. Can I see your phone for a second?"

"I must have left my phone on the counter in the kitchen at the donut shop," I said as I realized what I'd done.

"Well, let's go get it," Grace said as her own phone started to ring. She glanced at the number, and then she said, "It's my boss. I was hoping she wouldn't call me today, but this is going to take some time. I have files at the house that I'm going to have to reference for our conversation. Could you meet me at my place in half an hour? Don't do anything else without me, though. Promise?"

"I'll try not to," I said.

As Grace answered the phone and hurried up the road toward her house, I headed back to the donut shop. Crossing the street, I couldn't help but wonder why the frame had been so poorly executed. It didn't sound as though it was something Alexa might do. She struck me as being extremely competent, and what was more, I doubted she would have chosen that book so clumsily. No, it felt as though it was a last-second thought, a chance discovery when the killer had grabbed the murder weapon to use on the publisher.

And if that was true, it meant that Simon Gant was the real killer.

How could I prove it, though? I needed to call the police chief and bring him up to speed on my latest theory. Maybe, if I could point him in the right direction, he could figure out a way to trap Simon. At least in my mind, if the police chief had the killer's identity, he could dig in and see where it led him. If Chief Grant refused to listen to my idea, then Grace and I could always just do it ourselves.

I went into the donut shop after unlocking the front door, and I thought about locking it behind me, but then I decided not to bother when I realized I'd only be inside for a few seconds. Grabbing my phone from the kitchen exactly where I'd left it, I picked it up and dialed the chief's number.

It went straight to voicemail.

When it was time to leave a message, I said, "Chief, it's Suzanne. You need to look at the one author who writes mysteries without plotting them out first. It's…"

I stopped in mid-sentence when I saw that someone had used my carelessness against me and had followed me into Donut Hearts without me knowing they were there.

Simon Gant was standing in front of me with a knife taken from the drying rack, and as he reached out to take my phone before I could name him, I realized that I'd just made my final, and perhaps fatal, mistake.

CHAPTER 20

"**Y**OU MUST THINK YOU'RE PRETTY clever," Simon said as he took my cell phone from my hand. "How long have you known that I did it?"

"Honestly? I'm embarrassed to say that I just now figured it out," I admitted. "But that doesn't mean that everyone else won't be able to work it out for themselves just the same as I did."

"I'm curious about something. Where exactly did I slip up? At the time, it seemed like the perfect murder to me," he said. Simon was closer than I would have liked, and I didn't have any real weapons at hand. The oil had cooled off enough not to scald him, and he was standing between me and the other knives on the rack. The only thing within reach was a pair of rolling donut cutters, and they weren't exactly blunt instruments. Made of aluminum and maple, I doubted they weighed more than three pounds apiece.

Not exactly the perfect weapon to defend myself, but what other choice did I have? I needed to keep him talking, though. If I delayed him from acting long enough, the chief might start to wonder about my message. I didn't expect him to come by Donut Hearts directly, but if he called me back, it might offer enough distraction to allow me to grab one of the cutters and at least try to defend myself.

"Really, you were pretty clever," I said, trying to stoke the man's ego enough to buy myself more time.

"Why is that?" he asked, the knife dipping a little as he looked interested in what I had to say.

"If someone had planned it out meticulously, they would have taken one of Brad's books and placed it beside the body, but you used a title with 'deadly' in its name. It gave a feeling of credibility to the situation."

"That was more by circumstance than guile," he said. "I thought about doing just that, but all of Brad's books were up front, and I couldn't take the chance that someone might look through the window and see me taking one. I'd spotted the mushroom book when I'd grabbed the bookend, so it seemed close enough to work."

"Using the wrong hand was a bit of a gaff, though," I said.

It was clearly a mistake pointing it out to him. Simon clouded up, and the knife seemed to move toward me of its own volition.

"Can you believe it? I never noticed that the fool was left-handed," he said.

"Anyone could have made the same mistake," I answered, doing my best to mollify him again. It wouldn't do to anger him if I could help it. Apparently, when Simon felt threatened, even by my words, he became more aggressive toward me. "I'm curious about something, though. Why did you use the bookend? There were plenty of other blunt objects around you could have used."

"I'd like to say that it was symbolic of the bookends of my career, and his life, but the truth is that it was the first heavy thing I saw." The madman actually grinned at me. "If I were writing it, I'd use the symbols, though."

"You should turn the whole thing into one of your suspense novels," I said. "Think how clever you'll feel when no one guesses that you're really outlining a murder that you actually committed." Where was the police chief, and more importantly, why hadn't he at least called me back? "Speaking of which, why did you kill John? Was it because he was dropping you?"

"No, not in and of itself. That was bad enough, but I asked him to at least revert the rights of my books back to me if he wasn't going to publish them anymore, but he just laughed at me. He said that he'd print one copy a year of each title, which was all that he was legally required to do to keep the rights, just to ruin my life. Then he told me that I couldn't even use my own characters to write more books in the series without him! If I had to start over from scratch, then I knew that I was ruined. My career would be over. I still can't believe my agent let that clause stand. The more I think about it, after I leave here, I'm heading straight for New York. She needs to be the next one on my list," he said with wicked satisfaction. It appeared that once he'd gotten a taste of murder, he'd grown to like it. It gave me just one more reason to try to stop him before he could kill again, especially since I was the next victim on his list.

"Why did you flip the breaker and yet leave the front door open?" I asked him, trying to come up with some way to keep stalling him.

"I thought it might muddy the waters a little more, and besides, I knew Paige would find the body soon enough. Why not make it more of a game?"

I was about to answer when suddenly my cell phone rang in Simon's free hand.

It was time to act!

Lunging for the nearest donut cutter, I realized that I had less than a second to pick it up and try to defend myself.

For a portly older man, Simon Gant was really quick!

When I looked back at him, I saw that the knife was closer to my chest than I could have imagined, and it appeared that my plan to fight back might just be a case of too little too late.

CHAPTER 21

I N DESPERATION, I SWUNG THE cutter out anyway, and by some stroke of luck, one of the aluminum rings managed to catch the knife blade before it could plunge into my heart. Both weapons clattered to the floor as they got tangled up together, but the battle wasn't over yet, not by a long shot.

If Simon had gone for my throat with his hands, I would have been a dead woman, but instead, he reached down for the knife.

For an instant I thought about trying to fight him for it, but then I realized that I would probably lose that battle.

However, there was still one donut cutter within reach.

I grabbed it, and, swinging it with all that I had, I brought it crashing down onto the crown of his head.

It didn't knock him out, but it did manage to stagger him back a bit.

When I saw that, I did what anyone would do, given the circumstances.

I hit him again.

That blow managed to daze him considerably, and I was about to hit him again for good measure when I heard the chief of police say, "Take it easy, Suzanne. I think that's good enough."

I let the antique cutter fall to the floor once I realized that I was safe.

Donuts, or more specifically the tools I used to make them, had once again somehow managed to save my life.

CHAPTER 22

"A RE YOU OKAY?" JAKE ASKED me an hour later as I sat in one of the police chief's chairs in his office. I leapt out of my chair and embraced him, happy to have the chance to feel his arms around me once more. It turned out that Simon Gant had broken down and confessed everything once the cuffs had been slapped on. The chief had gotten my interrupted message, and he had rushed over, ready to save the day.

Only I'd already managed to save it, though I appreciated the fact that he'd come when he had. He was conferring with Grace in the other room, and my husband had found me sitting alone in his former office. "I heard about it on the way over here," he said as he stroked my back lightly.

"I would have called, but they won't give me my phone back," I said as I hugged him again. I always loved my husband's embrace, but none had ever felt as good as this one. I thought I'd been finished, but here I was, living and breathing and ready to make donuts again and to fight another day.

"What happened with Terry?"

"No worries on that front. We found her, safe and sound. She's a little worse for the wear, but she's going to be okay."

"And the man who was holding her?" I asked, a hitch in my voice.

"He's in jail." I let out of sigh of relief, and Jake asked, "What were you expecting?"

"I was afraid that you might have hurt him," I confessed.

"He might have gotten a few bumps and bruises before we could make the arrest, but hey, he shouldn't have taken a swing at Terry, not after what he'd done." Jake seemed rather pleased with himself, and I wasn't about to try to steal his thunder. He was back with me, and safe, and that was all that really mattered to me.

I decided to tell him exactly that. "I'm glad you're okay."

"From the sound of it, I was safer than you were," he said. "I was never in any real danger at all."

"What can I say? I seem to attract trouble like a magnet."

"Let's see what we can do about changing that," he said.

"Funny you should say that. I'm starting to think that maybe I've pressed my luck one too many times investigating these murders."

"I don't blame you for feeling that way a bit. By the way, the chief said you were free to go, since you've already signed your statement. What do you say we get out of here and grab something to eat? I'm starving."

I realized that I was hungry as well. "How about Napoli's? Can you wait until we get to Union Square?" I asked, mentioning our favorite restaurant.

"You know I'm never going to say no to that," Jake answered with a grin.

As we made our way to the restaurant, I thought about what I'd told Jake in the police chief's office. Was it time to step back from investigating murders, or was I just still a little shaky from my confrontation with Simon Gant? Could I really give it up if murder crossed my path again sometime in the future? At this point I couldn't say for sure, and only time would tell if a murder ever came my way again.

But in the meantime, I decided to enjoy every last bit of life I had in me.

"I've been thinking about taking some time off from the donut shop and going on an extended vacation. What do you think about that?"

"Let's swing by the house before we go eat. If you can give me twenty minutes to pack, I'll be ready to go," Jake said with a grin.

"Wow, are you sure you don't want some time to think about it first?" I asked with a smile of my own.

"I don't even care where we go. Let's just get out of town and see where the road takes us."

"It's a deal. I'm sure Emma and Sharon will be happy to take over for as long as we need them."

"Then it's set," he said. "After we eat, we can decide which way to head: north, south, east, and west. It doesn't matter a bit to me, as long as we're together."

"I can hardly wait," I replied. "I'll make the phone calls I need to make after we pack and start driving to Napoli's. You still want to go there, right?"

"Well, we have to eat anyway, don't we?" he asked me with a grin.

It was the answer I'd been counting on.

I wasn't sure where the days ahead might lead us, but one thing was certain.

If I had Jake with me, then I had all that I really needed in the world, and at least for a little while, Donut Hearts would be fine without me.

RECIPES

Fun and Easy Rainy-Day Donuts

I call these rainy-day donuts because sometimes when the kids are out of school and you've done every last single arts and crafts project, you need something to fill your time until dinner. I love these donuts because they are airy and light with just a tad of sweetness. I specifically like the fact that the dough just has to go through one rise cycle instead of two, so the next time the rain is pouring down outside, or your kids are just a little bored, give these a try!

Ingredients

- 2 packages fast-rising yeast (1⁄2 ounce total)
- 1 cup water, warm
- 2 1⁄2 tablespoons granulated sugar
- 1 egg, beaten
- 1⁄3 cup butter or margarine, melted
- 1 teaspoon cinnamon
- 1 teaspoon nutmeg
- 1 teaspoon vanilla extract
- 1⁄2 teaspoon salt
- 3–4 cups flour

Directions

In a large bowl, mix the yeast, water, and sugar together. In about five minutes, the yeast will start to work. Add the beaten egg, melted butter, cinnamon, nutmeg, vanilla, and salt, blend it all together thoroughly, then start adding flour ½ a cup at a time until the dough is no longer sticky to the touch. Turn the dough out onto a floured board and knead it for about a minute, then roll the dough out with a rolling pin until it's approximately 1/4 to 1/2 inch thick. After you've done that, cut out whatever donut shapes, diamonds, or ravioli-cutter shapes please you. This is a good time to get the kids involved, and it doesn't really matter if the shapes are perfect or not.

Set these aside to rise for half an hour, and then fry them in 360°F canola oil, turning once so both sides cook evenly. Don't crowd them while they're cooking or the oil temperature will drop too quickly.

After the donuts are golden brown, drain them on paper towels. You can eat them plain, dust them with powdered sugar, or even make your own icing. This is another time to let the kids get involved, personalizing their own treats with sprinkles and other confections.

Makes 6 to 10 donuts, depending on the shapes you select.

Baked Fruit-Flavored Donuts

If you're craving a donut but you don't want to fry it in oil, baked donuts offer a delicious alternative. I've been playing with several baked recipes for years, and some of them are quite tasty. You can use a donut pan in your oven or even buy a standalone donut baker, which I love using! Either way, have fun, and don't be afraid to experiment. That's how this recipe came to be when I had a yearning for something different.

Ingredients

- Wet
- 1 egg, beaten slightly
- 1/2 cup whole milk (2% can be substituted.)
- 1/2 cup granulated white sugar
- 1 tablespoon butter, melted (I use unsalted; salted can be used, but cut the added salt by half.)
- 1 teaspoon vanilla extract

Dry

- 1 cup all-purpose flour (I prefer unbleached, but bleached is fine, and so is bread flour.)
- 1 teaspoon baking powder
- 1 teaspoon baking soda
- 1/2 teaspoon salt
- 1/2 cup dried fruit (any combination of fruit bits like raisins, cranberry, apple, apricot, plum, peach, cherry)

Directions

Combine all of the listed dry ingredients together except the fruit, adding the flour, baking powder, baking soda, and salt in a bowl and sifting them all together thoroughly. In another bowl, combine the wet ingredients by mixing together the beaten egg, milk, sugar, butter, and vanilla extract. Slowly add the contents of the bowl containing the wet mix directly to the dry, stirring it all in until it's incorporated, but try not to over-mix. Lastly, coat the fruit pieces with a teaspoon of flour to keep them suspended in the batter, add the fruit to the batter and mix it lightly in.

It's really that simple. Now they are ready to bake. Set your oven to 350° and bake them for 10 to 15 minutes. You can use cupcake trays, small donut molds, or, if you have a countertop donut baker, set the timer for 6 to 7 minutes, or until the donuts are golden.

I like these plain, since they have a good amount of fruit already in them, but you can dust them with powdered sugar or make a simple fruit glaze by reducing your favorite fruit jam by half on the stovetop.

Makes 6 to 8 donuts.

The Donut That's Not Really a Donut!

This recipe was born out of desperation and an unwillingness on my part to create a lot of dirty dishes! There is some debate in my house that this even qualifies as a recipe, but I've yet to see a single member of my family turn down one of these delightful treats, especially when they come out hot and steaming. The results are impressive, and they are so easy to make, how can you not try them just once?

Ingredients

- 1 can biscuit dough (I like the sourdough recipe)
- Any toppings you may desire

Directions

Pop open the can and separate the biscuits. You can use your donut-hole cutter to remove the centers, or fry them intact. Drop the rounds into canola oil that's been heated to 375°F. Turn after 2 minutes so they cook on each side. If you choose to produce rounds, don't forget to fry the holes, as they are equally delightful.

Drain your donuts on a rack or on paper towels, and after they've cooled slightly, dust them with powdered sugar, cocoa powder, or even make your own sugary glaze.

Makes 4 to 8 donuts.

If you enjoy Jessica Beck Mysteries and you would like to be notified when the next book is being released, please send your email address to **newreleases@jessicabeckmysteries.net**. Your email address will not be shared, sold, bartered, traded, broadcast, or disclosed in any way. There will be no spam from us, just a friendly reminder when the latest book is being released.

Also, be sure to visit our website at jessicabeckmysteries.net for valuable information about Jessica's books.

OTHER BOOKS BY JESSICA BECK

The Ghost Cat Cozy Mysteries
Ghost Cat: Midnight Paws
Ghost Cat 2: Bid for Midnight

The Cast Iron Cooking Mysteries
Cast Iron Will
Cast Iron Conviction
Cast Iron Alibi
Cast Iron Motive
Cast Iron Suspicion

Made in the USA
San Bernardino, CA
17 April 2017